five
minutes
more

five minutes more

Darlene Ryan

ORCA BOOK PUBLISHERS

Library and Archives Canada Cataloguing in Publication

Ryan, Darlene, 1958-
Five minutes more / written by Darlene Ryan.

ISBN 978-1-55469-006-0

I. Title.

PS8635.Y35F59 2009   jC813'.6   C2008-907416-5

First published in the United States, 2009
Library of Congress Control Number: 2008941139

Summary: After D'Arcy's father dies, she struggles to come to terms with the fact that he committed suicide.

Orca Book Publishers gratefully acknowledges the support for its publishing programs provided by the following agencies: the Government of Canada through the Book Publishing Industry Development Program and the Canada Council for the Arts, and the Province of British Columbia through the BC Arts Council and the Book Publishing Tax Credit.

Cover and text design by Teresa Bubela
Typesetting by Christine Toller
Cover artwork by Getty Images
Author photo by Kevin Ryan

ORCA BOOK PUBLISHERS
PO Box 5626, STN. B
VICTORIA, BC CANADA
V8R 6S4

ORCA BOOK PUBLISHERS
PO Box 468
CUSTER, WA USA
98240-0468

www.orcabook.com
Printed and bound in Canada.
Printed on 100% PCW recycled paper.
12 11 10 09 • 4 3 2 1

For Susan

Part One

Autumn

one

I play the Five Minutes More game. Five minutes. I can stand anything for five minutes. Even my father being dead.

We're making the *arrangements*. Nobody has used the word *funeral*. My mother's answering questions for the announcement that will be in the newspaper. Her hands are folded in her lap, one hand over the other. She seems so calm and in control. Only I can see that on the bottom hand—the hidden one—she's picking at the side of her thumb with the nail of her middle finger, so a patch of raw, sore skin is exposed. She sees me looking at her and she gives me a little smile that's really just lips stretching, and I give it right back because I don't know what else to do.

Five minutes.

Mom and Mr. Rosborough are standing up now, so I get up too. "And no visitation," she says, smoothing her skirt.

"Of course," he murmurs.

Mr. Rosborough is the funeral director. He's very tall and thin, with lots of white hair combed back from his forehead. He's wearing a dark blue suit and tie with a very white shirt. His skin is very white too, and he has deep hollows below his cheekbones, as though his face is just skin and bone and nothing else. He looks exactly how I would have expected a funeral director to look if I had ever actually thought about it before today.

His doorplate only says *Director*. I guess nobody uses the word *undertaker*. Anyway, *director* seems like the right word to me. I feel as though I've walked onstage in the middle of a play. I'm just trying to stay out of the way until I can figure out how to get off again.

We go up to the second floor. I trail my hand up the banister. The wood is smooth and dark with age. This used to be someone's house. People lived here.

The top of the stairs opens into a big room, and the whole space is full of coffins.

Everywhere.

My breath sticks in my chest. I hear myself make a sucking sound halfway between a gasp and a heave, but no one else seems to notice. There's nowhere to look and not see the coffins. They're hanging from the ceiling, mounted on the walls, displayed on stands in rows like some kind of death department store. There's polished wood, metals that gleam like new change, velour and even some kind of white vinyl with studs that looks like it was recycled from an old car seat.

I close my eyes, but the image of the room is printed on the inside of my eyelids in swirling colors, like some kind of psychedelic negative. I open them again and try to take a deep breath.

Five minutes more, I tell myself. Five minutes was what my dad said when I didn't want to get a needle or go to the dentist. It's what he said when I hid under my bed on the first day of kindergarten.

"Five minutes. Then, if you don't want to stay, we'll go for French fries." And if I wanted to leave when the five minutes were up, he'd say, "We're already here. Let's just stay for five more minutes, and if you want to leave after that we'll go get those fries."

My dad could five-minutes-more me through almost anything. And after, we always ended up at Fern's Diner sharing a big plate of fries with gravy on an oversized yellow pressed-paper plate.

"D'Arcy." My mother motions me over to her.

"I think you'll be very satisfied with this," Mr. Rosborough says, as though we were going to take the...thing home with us.

Up close he gives off the scent of flowers and something else that seems familiar but that I can't identify. The smell is sticky. It makes my head throb. I start to breathe through my mouth and try not to think about what that smell could be.

"What do you think?" Mom asks. The one they're standing beside is storm-cloud gray with some kind of space-age polymer finish. The inside is lined with a shiny blue ruffled fabric, like a tacky tuxedo shirt.

Little sparkles of light are dancing around the edges of my vision. Yesterday my dad drove his car into the river that runs beside the old highway. How am I supposed to answer?

"It's nice," I tell her.

We drive home in the dark, spits of rain hitting the windshield. The wipers click on, *snick snick* across the glass, pause and then do it again. I need some answers—I just don't know how to ask her the questions

"Did he leave a letter or anything?" I jump, realizing I've finally said it out loud. Now the words are out, I keep going. "How can they know for sure that he...?"

I watch my mother without turning my head. She takes a quick look in the rearview mirror, and then her eyes go back to the road. She never looks at me. "There's no letter," she says finally. "The car went into the river. The rest is nobody's business."

The only sound is the wipers moving across the glass in front of me. My mother doesn't say anything more. And neither do I.

*⁎⁎

"D'Arcy, there's a plastic garment bag somewhere in the hall closet. It's probably on the shelf or at the back. Would you get it for me, please?" Mom asks.

There's a long black bag on a hook behind the coats. I take it upstairs. "Is this what you wanted?" I ask from the bedroom doorway.

"That's it." She takes the bag and opens the zipper. "Does this smell okay to you?"

I nod. I can't go into the room.

Mom has laid out my dad's underwear on the bed: a white T-shirt, dark socks and a pair of those stupid boxer shorts he liked. They have green smiley faces on them.

No.

"Rocky and Bullwinkle," I say.

She turns. "What?"

I point at the stuff on the bed. "Rocky and Bullwinkle." She gets it then, pulls open a drawer and moves things around until she finds the right underwear.

"I thought maybe the gray pinstripe," she says, bringing the suit from the closet.

My father wasn't really a suit person, but what difference does it make? He's not going anywhere in it. I'm pretty sure suggesting jeans with holes in them would be wrong.

So I nod again. My head still hurts. Maybe I'm getting the flu or something.

The suit's in the bag now, along with a pale blue shirt. Mom holds up a red and navy striped tie. "I think this one." She folds the tie and the underwear into the pocket at the bottom of the garment bag. Then she turns to me. "D'Arcy, go put the kettle on, please. I could use a cup of something hot. I'll be right down."

In the kitchen I fill the kettle, set it on to boil and drop two peppermint tea bags in the china pot. When Mom turned forty-five she gave up caffeine. Now she drinks herbal tea—peppermint, chamomile and rose hip.

I lean on the counter for a minute, but I can't stay still. I know in a few minutes the phone will ring or someone will be at the door.

I go upstairs again. Through the half-open bedroom door I can see Mom. She's sitting on the end of the bed with the bag on her lap. Her hand is tracing slow circles on the plastic. I feel as though I'm watching something private that I shouldn't be seeing. I back away from the door.

two

I wake up five or six times during the night from strange dreams I can't really remember. I end up sleeping later than I wanted to, and when I get up I feel as though I didn't go to bed at all.

It's the first time since Mom and I got back from the funeral home that we've been alone in the house for more than a few minutes. Someone else is always here, putting food on a plate, patting me on the arm and looking sad.

A car pulls into the driveway. Mom's at the table in the dining room. "She's here," I say. Mom gets up, glancing at her watch. We go into the kitchen in time to hear the soft knock on the door before it opens.

It's Claire. My sister. My half-sister to be exact. There's no way anyone can make that half into a real sister for me.

She's carrying her coat with a tote bag over one shoulder. Her eyes make a circuit around the kitchen; then she says, "Hello." She doesn't look like she's been driving for hours.

She doesn't look like her father just died. She looks perfect because that's Claire. Her short blond hair shines like a shampoo commercial. She's wearing navy check pants and a creamy sweater. I don't think she owns jeans. And I bet if she put on a sweatshirt, she'd break out in a rash.

"Claire. I'm glad you're here," Mom says. Her hands move, start to reach out, but then she pulls back and clasps them in front of her.

"Leah," Claire says. She looks at me. "Hello, D'Arcy."

"You must be tired. Can I get you anything? Are you hungry? There's lots of food," Mom says. I want to tell her to stop talking.

"No. I stopped to eat about an hour ago. What I'd really like is more details. You didn't say much on the telephone."

Details. What does she mean? The car went into the river. Dad's dead. The end.

I see my mother tense her shoulders. "Of course," she says. "We should go over the arrangements of the service as well."

"You already planned the service." The way Claire says the words, it sounds like my mother did something wrong.

"Yes. I'm sorry I couldn't wait until you got here." Their eyes lock. Mom looks away first. "Why don't you put your things upstairs? Then we'll talk."

"Fine," Claire says. "How are you, D'Arcy?" she asks as she passes me.

"I'm all right," I say back. I may as well have said "aardvark." If you say something over and over, the way I've said "I'm all right" in the past twenty-four hours, it stops making any sense.

As Claire goes by, her hand reaches out. I'm surprised to feel the prickle of tears in my eyes and throat. Claire was ten when I was born. In all my life I don't think she's ever hugged me, not even when I was a baby. I uncross my arms, start to open my body. She pushes the hair away from my face and moves by.

I jerk my head back as though I've been smacked. I don't think she notices. She's done that to my hair for as long as I can remember, the only times I think we've touched. Claire doesn't like my hair. It's long and blond and it curls wherever it wants to. Like Dad's. Not like hers. Claire could be in the middle of a hurricane and not get messed up. It's like there's a bubble around her so she stays neat and perfect.

I'm standing at the living room window when my mother comes downstairs. I hear her behind me, but I don't turn around. I don't want to talk. It won't help. We watch a squirrel bury a nut in the leaves around the rose bushes. I know he'll probably forget and never come back for it.

Mom touches my shoulder. "Are you okay?"

"Why did she have to come?"

"He's her father too."

"I don't care. She never came when he was…here." I fold the edge of the curtain into little pleats.

"D'Arcy, she's your sister," Mom says sharply.

"She's my half-sister. Half. It's not the same. It's not like a real sister."

Mom grabs my shoulder and swings me around. "Listen to me. Claire is your sister. Your real sister. We don't divide people into halves and quarters. I know, *I know*, that she's not

9

the easiest person to get along with, but we're going to try. It was very important to your father." She lets me go, lets out a breath and clenches her hands into tight fists. "Please?"

I don't want to. Don't try to tell me Claire is my real sister. I'm not even sure she's a real person.

I want to shout that at Mom, but I stop myself. I look back out the window. The squirrel, finished hiding nuts for now, runs up a tree, stopping and starting in jerky motion. It's how I think I probably look when I move. It's how I feel.

I turn around to face my mother. There are tiny lines in her face that I haven't seen before. It's only a couple of days. This will be over. Claire will be gone. Then everything will be back to normal. I can do this.

"All right," I say.

three

We're ready early for the service. I look out my bedroom window before I head downstairs. It's damp and dark. I can't even see the big oak tree where my swing used to be. Fog smothers the yard and seems to be pushing at the windows, trying to take over the house too.

We sit in the living room, on the edge of our seats so we don't wrinkle. Except Claire. Claire doesn't wrinkle. She's the only one in black—a dress that looks expensive and probably is. I wonder if she bought it for this.

Mom is wearing her dark blue suit. I notice she has a bandage on her thumb. She keeps getting up to answer the door and coming back with another casserole or a plate of brownies. Why would anyone think that would help? How can pasta spirals and crabmeat make a difference?

I pick microscopic bits of lint off my green skirt. My hair is twisted back in a fancy ponytail. Claire did it. She stood

11

in the doorway of my room and said, "I'll do your hair." Not "can I, may I, do you want me to?" My mouth was open to say no, and then I remembered I'd said I'd try with Claire, and I thought, *Maybe she's trying with me. Maybe now we'll be sisters.* You'd think I'd know better. How many times have I thought that before? All Claire wanted was to get my hair out of my face.

We all seem to decide at the same time that we should leave. We take Claire's car. I'm surprised at how much traffic there is, how many people I see. Everybody's just going on with their lives like nothing happened. But then, to them, nothing has.

Mr. Rosborough is waiting for us. Today he's wearing a black suit with another of those blinding white shirts. I wonder how he keeps the lint off that suit. Maybe his wife brushes it for him every night. Maybe she wraps tape around her hand, sticky side out, and takes off every speck and thread.

Mr. Rosborough takes us to the Chapel of Ease so we can "look things over." The casket is at the front of the room with a big spray of red and white carnations on top. I won't think about what's inside.

There are way too many flowers in the room. Dad says flowers are wasted on dead people. Doesn't anyone remember? This is wrong. I turn to tell Mom, but she's kneeling on a padded step in front of all those flowers. She rests her hand next to the carnations. Claire's just standing there, so I kneel too. I don't want to, but it looks wrong, my mother on her knees by herself. I lower my head so I'm looking at the carpet and lace my fingers tightly in front of me. There's no way I'm putting my hand up there.

As Mom stands up she touches my cheek. Her hand is freezing. Her hands are always cold. "Cold hands, warm heart," she'd always say when my dad would tell her that there were corpses with warmer hands. But I don't want to think about that either.

As I get up, Mr. Rosborough is saying something about the lounge. Mom shakes her head. Her voice is low, so I can't hear what she tells him, but I guess that she wants to stay in this room.

"I don't think that's necessary, Leah," Claire says in her cool voice.

"No, Claire, I don't suppose that you would," Mom answers. Her voice is still quiet, but everyone hears her. Then she turns to me, "D'Arcy will stay with me, won't you?"

No. I don't want to do this. I don't want to stay in this room, with that box, with what used to be my father, but how can I say no? Five minutes. I'll stay here for five minutes. But not one second more.

I nod.

We sit on a bench, close to the door. It's a lot like a church pew, which means you have to sit up straight and it's not very comfortable. Mom sits with her back as rigid as the back of her seat, her hands folded in her lap—no picking at her thumbs today. I can't look where she's looking, so I study the flowers closest to me. Mostly there are lilies and carnations. Serious flowers.

I don't like the lilies. Their smell sticks in the back of my nose. I know I'll still smell it days from now.

I touch Mom's arm. She jerks and looks at me as though she'd forgotten I was there. "These flowers, don't you think they're wrong?" I ask. "I mean, he wouldn't like this. I don't understand why people sent them. Didn't anyone pay attention to what was in the paper?"

"They're beautiful, aren't they?" she says, getting up.

What? Didn't she hear me?

"I chose the carnations. I didn't think roses seemed right for a man. But the carnations, they even smell sort of spicy, like a man's aftershave." She runs her fingers lightly over the top of the blooms, ruffling the petals.

I don't know what to say now. I'd like to run up there and rip the petals off every single flower. But I don't. I never do those kinds of things, except in my head. I want to ask Mom why she's acting like this. But I don't do that either. Maybe she thinks some of the things I'm doing and saying are strange too.

Then I'm saved from having to say or do anything because Brendan is in the doorway with his parents. I didn't know he owned a suit. I'm sure the tie is his dad's. And he had his hair cut. All the curly bits at the back of his neck that I like to twist around my fingers are gone.

Brendan takes one of my hands and squeezes it. I try to smile at him but it doesn't feel like the muscles in my face are working.

Mrs. Henderson hugs Mom. Mr. Henderson takes her hand, holding it between both of his.

"You all right?" Brendan whispers.

I nod. "I'm okay. It's just…It's just so weird."

"I know." But he doesn't. "Oh, I almost forgot." He pulls a pale blue envelope out of his pocket. "It's from Marissa. Her mom brought it over to my house. She's still sick."

Marissa's my best friend—the first friend I ever made, the second week of second grade. I take the envelope. Marissa thinks Brendan's a dumb jock. I get a lump in my throat, thinking about her worrying about me and sending her mom over to his house.

Brendan touches my arm. "Want me to stay with you?"

I do and I don't. Mostly I don't. I shake my head. "There isn't anything you can do. You're coming to the house, after, right?"

"Yeah."

"Good."

Brendan looks around and then kisses my forehead before he gives my hand one last squeeze. Mrs. Henderson gives me one of those lips-only smiles that everyone's been using since this all started.

There are more people coming in. Mom's hugging people and shaking hands, thanking everyone for coming as though this were some kind of party. I do the same thing, because as strange as it feels, it seems to be what you're supposed to do.

Every hand I shake, I look into the person's face and wonder what they know. It didn't say in the announcement in the paper. Maybe they think my dad had a heart attack while he was driving. I don't want anyone to know. Because it's not like we really know for sure. I don't want people talking about him and thinking he did something when nobody knows for sure that he did.

four

The seats are full. Mr. Rosborough and another dark-suited man set up folding chairs at the back. Claire comes in with a woman. Her mother. I've never met Claire's mother, but right away I'm sure of who it is. She is all cool and blond, like Claire. She's wearing a black suit and a little black hat with a veil.

Out of nowhere I feel intense hate for that stupid hat. Hate that makes my head ache, pushing at my forehead, trying to get out. I want to rip that hat off her head and stomp it flat.

My mother has gone over to them. She's talking to *her*, taking *her* hand. Mom turns, reaches for me, urging me over. "D'Arcy," she says. "This is Claire's mother."

"Hello," I say. I can't think of this person being married to my dad. He was funny. He laughed a lot. He made other people laugh. *She* doesn't look like she ever laughs.

"Hello, D'Arcy. I'm so sorry about your father."

I catch my hand starting to move for that hat. I make it touch Mom's arm instead.

"Elizabeth, sit with us. Please," Mom says.

Sit with us. I don't think so.

"I don't think so," *she* says.

Good.

"Please." Mom is insistent. "You're family."

She hesitates.

I don't want to sit next to *her* and that hat.

"All right. Thank you, Leah."

What's the matter with my mother? Is she crazy? I have this feeling that the world has tipped sideways, and I reach out for something to steady myself. This person is not family. Not ours. She's part of my father's life from before. The life he didn't want anymore.

At exactly two o'clock, we take our seats. Mom, me, Claire and *her*, all in that front seat.

The words of the service blur in my mind. I hear the minister say something about faith and God's plan for us. I let the words come into my head without paying attention to them. I'm not talking to God right now. Not talking. Not listening. He let this happen. I concentrate on breathing steadily. In and out. I'm not going to cry. I don't know why that's so important, but it is.

And then it's over. We're in the lounge waiting for everyone to leave the chapel. I sit by myself on a couch along the end wall. The cushions are too squishy. Mr. Rosborough is talking to my mother. I can't make out the words, but she's nodding. I think that's all we've done today, nod and mumble.

Mom comes across the room and sits on the edge of the couch next to me. "Are we going now?" I ask her.

"Not yet." She puts one of her hands over mine. It's still very cold. "D'Arcy, would you like to see him? Before we go."

I almost say, "See who?" But even as a part of my brain is thinking that, another part realizes that she's talking about my dad.

"He looks nice, D'Arcy. Just like he was sleeping."

I yank my hand away. He's dead. How can he look nice? *Don't think about it.*

"No," I say. My voice is loud. She looks hurt, but I can't care about that right now.

"All right. That's all right." She lifts a hand toward my face, then hesitates and pulls it back. "We'll be leaving soon," she says as she gets to her feet.

I watch her go over to Claire. I wonder if she's saying the same thing to her. Mom looks back at me then. I look away fast. I stare at the wallpaper. It's the same paper as in the chapel, some sort of fuzzy burgundy design like palm fronds. It looks like something that belongs in a restaurant.

Everything feels wrong. Ever since that police officer came to the door, it's as if real time, real life, has stopped. There's a whole piece of my life after that that's missing. I don't know what happened to it.

five

We drive home in silence. It's raining, big fat drops that splatter on the windshield like tears.

Almost everyone comes back to the house after the service. People have been bringing food for days. I'd wondered how we were ever going to eat it all. I don't think that's going to be a problem anymore.

There are trays of sandwiches with no crusts cut in fingers and little triangles and even perfectly round circles. There's a platter of ham and one of turkey. There are two kinds of coleslaw and three of potato salad, plus enough rolls for the minister to recreate the miracle of the loaves and fishes right here in our kitchen. At least the loaves part.

People keep trying to get me to have something, but I can't eat. I don't know how anybody can eat anything. I can't swallow. I think if I did actually eat anything, it would just fall off the back of my tongue into emptiness.

A couple of women from Mom's office have taken over the kitchen. I see people hugging my mother, saying things that are supposed to be comforting, but aren't—not to me. I wander between the kitchen and the living room, always moving so I won't have to talk to anyone. I hear pieces of conversations; it's like switching between channels on a TV.

"...I think he's left her fairly well off. He must have gotten something when his own father died."

"...had every right. She was married to him first."

"...couldn't do anything with his face."

Suddenly I can't stand it anymore. Not for five minutes. Not for one minute. No one's looking at me. With my back to the kitchen door, I turn the knob and slip through into the porch.

An old sweater of my dad's is hanging on a hook by the outside door. His boots sit on a fold of newspaper underneath. One points straight ahead, the other off to one side, as though he had just been beamed out of them. I pull the sweater over my head. The bottom edge hits the middle of my thighs, and the sleeves hang below the ends of my fingers. I wrap my arms around my shoulders, close my eyes and bury my face in the crook of an elbow, breathing in his scent caught in the itchy brown wool. I pretend that it's him hugging me, and for a moment everything is the way that it was. Everything is all right.

I decide to give God another chance. *It's not supposed to be like this*, I tell him in my head. *Please. Make it the way it was.*

I wait for a moment and then open my eyes. I can hear everyone inside. Nothing's different.

It's stopped raining. I walk down behind the house, through the trees, to where the rock wall marks the end of our yard. The leaves are slippery under my feet. I kick at a small pile of them. They make a soggy sound and one big oak leaf sticks to the toe of my shoe. The two maples still hold most of their leaves. But they've already turned scarlet and bright buttery yellow. I know in a few days they'll be on the ground too.

I brush off a spot on the top of the wall and sit down. The stone is damp and its coldness pushes through the sweater and my skirt, but right now that's better than being in the house.

I pull out Marissa's note, tear open the envelope and read what she's written. She's sorry. Everyone's sorry. I fold the envelope and the paper in half and put them back in my pocket.

After a while I hear someone coming. I can't get away from people today. I think about jumping over the wall, but my shoes wouldn't be up to that. Then I see it's Brendan. I forgot all about him.

"I was looking for you," he says, stopping in front of me.

"I just had to get out for a little while. I needed…air. All those people, all that food. I couldn't breathe."

"Why didn't you come get me?"

I didn't even think about Brendan. I just wanted to get out. But I can't say that. "I didn't know where you were," I say. That much is true.

He puts his arm around me, and I put my head on his shoulder with my cheek against the smooth fabric of his suit jacket. "How can people eat?" I ask him. "How can they stand there and say how bad they feel and shovel in potato salad at the same time?"

He shrugs. "I don't know. Maybe they don't know what else to do."

"It's like one of those dreams where nothing makes sense. You know it's a dream, but you can't wake up."

"Yeah. I know it doesn't seem real. Your dad was a good driver."

My heart is pounding so hard I think for sure Brendan will hear it. I haven't told him. Every time I start to tell him what the police said, something else comes out of my mouth. And it's not really a lie because maybe they're wrong. Maybe it was just an accident.

Brendan pulls me against him and wraps both arms around me. "It's gonna be all right," he whispers. He rubs his chin against the top of my hair.

No, it isn't, but how can he understand that? How can anybody?

I mumble something. I have no idea what, but it can't have been too weird because Brendan just gives me another hug. I press harder into his arms and try to get some of his warmth into me.

"Hey, you're shaking." He touches my face. "Jeez, D'Arcy, you're freezing. C'mon. You'll be sick if you stay out here much longer. You don't have to go back inside. We can sit in the car."

I look up at him. I see the way he's holding his mouth, how muscles in his jaw pop out because he's grinding his back teeth. He wants everybody to be happy all the time.

"It's okay," I say. "I should go in."

"You sure?"

"I'm sure."

Brendan walks me back to the house. His parents are by their car across the street, talking to another couple.

"You better go," I say.

"I don't have to."

I love him, but I don't want to watch him worry about me. I pull the cuffs of my dad's sweater down over my fingers. "I'm really tired. It's okay. You go home."

He studies my face for a moment. "All right. I'll call you later though." He kisses me quickly on the mouth. "I love you," he says.

I nod.

In the porch I hang the sweater back on its hook and straighten my father's boots so they're both facing forward. I take a deep breath. I can do this. I just won't think about any of it for now.

six

Inside, everyone's gone. Mom's in the kitchen, stacking dirty plates on the counter. She half turns when I walk in. "D'Arcy, there you are. Where have you been?"

"I haven't been anywhere. I just went outside for a minute to get some air."

It's only half a lie, which I guess is better than a whole one. Maybe not to God though. Maybe he keeps track of all the half lies, adds them up, and pretty soon you're in just as much trouble as if you'd been telling whole lies. I don't care if that's how God works. He may not like what I've been doing, but I don't like what he's been doing lately either.

Mom is gathering glasses and cups. "Sit, Mom," I say, steering her toward the table. I have to do better. "I'll do these."

"I don't mind," she says.

"No. Sit. I'm going to put the kettle on and make you a cup of tea."

"I think there's some left. I can have that."

I touch the pot. "You can't drink that. It's cold. Besides, it's the hard stuff." She almost manages a smile.

I fill the kettle and set it on a back burner. When I turn she's on her feet again, picking up crumpled napkins from the table. "Mom, I'll do that in a minute. C'mon, sit. Please?" I toss the napkins in the trash. "Take a break, okay?"

"I just want to get the kitchen cleaned up."

"I'll do it."

"All right. All right. I don't want to argue." She sits, slumping against the chair back.

"Where's Claire?" I ask.

Mom rests one elbow on the table and pulls her fingers through her hair. I notice how thin her face seems, how her cheekbones—which I didn't inherit and have always longed for—seem about to poke through the skin. "She's lying down."

She looks at me as though she expects me to say something. I bite my tongue. Literally. Claire will be gone tomorrow anyway.

I finish stacking the dishes and cram the last of the garbage into the bag. Then I make peppermint tea. While it steeps, I wash and dry a cup. I can feel my mother's eyes on me.

"What about you, D'Arcy? Are you all right?" she asks.

"I'm okay," I say as I hand her the tea. Another half lie, if anyone's counting. She presses both hands around the cup as though she's trying to draw its heat into her fingers. Her whole body seems to sag over the table.

I turn back to the sink. "Where's the car?" I ask.

"It's still across the street in the Keefers' driveway. I'll go get it in a minute."

"No." I have to stop and swallow because the words suddenly stick in my throat. "I mean Dad's car. Where is it?"

"The police still have it."

Keep going. "So they're still...investigating?"

"Yes..." She pulls a hand back through her hair. "Maybe. I don't know."

I keep rinsing cups under the hot water. "I think it was an accident. I really do."

It's a long time before my mother says anything. "Sometimes you don't get the answers you're looking for," she says. She gets up, comes behind me and squeezes my shoulders. "I'm sorry. Sometimes there aren't any answers."

*

The door to Claire's room is open. I catch sight of a photograph lying on the end of the bed. Water's running in the bathroom. One step and suddenly, somehow, I'm in the room.

In the picture a little blond girl is riding on the shoulders of a man. There's ice cream or something all over her face. They're both laughing, heads together, squinting into the sun as the wind blows their hair.

My father. And Claire.

I look at the picture again. They look...happy. I never really thought about my dad being happy in another life. I never thought about him playing with Claire, carrying her on his shoulders. I never really thought of Claire as a little girl.

Something squirms inside me. I drop the picture back on the bed, slip into the hall and go to my own room.

seven

12:26.

I can't sleep. The streetlight shines through the window, outlining the panes on the floor in weird, orange-pink light, like some special effect in a horror movie.

I roll over onto my back and listen to the creaks and snaps the house makes as it settles down for the night.

I was seven when we moved here. Back then the whole house scared me. It seemed so old, full of groans and squeaks and other strange noises. In the living room the wall-paper had come loose in long strips that always seemed to be moving, reaching out for me. Chunks of plaster would suddenly drop from the ceilings. And the backyard was an overgrown hunting ground for the neighborhood cats. But Dad turned fixing up this place into an adventure. He'd tell me stories about a mouse named Xavier who'd been packed by mistake in a tea chest and ended up at our house.

12:36.

I still can't sleep. My mind refuses to shut off. It keeps going places I have to pull it back from. I take slow deep breaths, trying to trick my brain into dozing off.

12:43.

If I take any more deep breaths I'm going to pass out. My stomach makes a sound like there's someone inside moaning, half starved, for food. I can't remember if I ate any supper.

I creep downstairs, placing each foot carefully, avoiding all the squeaky places on the stairs. I don't want to wake up my mom. I don't want to wake up Claire.

And then I hear voices. My heart begins to pound in double time. I listen. It's my mother. And Claire.

I press myself against the wall and move through the dining room to the living room doorway. I don't know why I'm hiding. The French doors are partly open. I lean around the doorframe and take a quick look through the closest pane of glass.

Mom is curled in the corner of the sofa, in a circle of light from a nearby lamp. She's wearing the plaid housecoat I gave her last Christmas. Claire is sitting in the wing chair, in a silky pink-flowered robe, perfect posture as usual.

"...just makes more sense to do it now," Claire is saying.

Mom seems to be looking beyond Claire. I lean a bit closer to the open doors to catch her voice.

"We just had your father's funeral today," she says. "I haven't been able to think beyond that. I'm not even sure about all the details of his will." She sounds very tired.

"The tea set belonged to my great-grandmother. I know my father would want me to have it. And as for the pearl necklace, you know that it's always stayed in the family."

"You're not the only person in the family."

"I don't think a teenager would have much use for a string of pearls."

"D'Arcy isn't going to be a teenager forever."

"In other words, you want everything for your child."

My dad's only been gone for a few days, and already they're fighting over his things.

"She's your sister, Claire," Mom says. "I'm not trying to cheat you out of anything, but I will not allow you to take things from this house until I know what your father wanted. I'll see that anything that's been left to you is sent. I wouldn't want you to have to make another trip."

"You're being unreasonable, Leah. My father—"

My mother's head snaps up. She's looking directly at Claire now. "*My husband* is dead. I'm entitled to be somewhat unreasonable." There is silence.

Claire's voice is low, and I almost miss that she's started talking. "And what kind of a wife were you, Leah? Didn't you notice what was going on with him or did you just not care? My father killed himself. Did you even try to help him?"

One of my mother's hands snaps up, and for a second I expect her to get up and slap Claire. Then the hand drops into her lap, the fingers pulled into a fist. I press the heel of my own hand over my mouth.

"You don't have a clue what was going on here. You didn't even know your father." My mother's voice is tight with anger. "Where the hell were you, Claire? Acting like a spoiled child because Mommy and Daddy got divorced. You wouldn't come to see him or spend any time with us. Do you know how much you hurt him? And he never stopped trying with you. You weren't much of a daughter, Claire."

Mom lets out a breath. "My husband's things stay in my husband's home until I know what he wants me to do with them. Good night, Claire." She puts her head back against the sofa and closes her eyes.

Claire gets up, and in a minute I hear the flap of her slippers going upstairs.

I rub my eyes with the back of my hand and swallow the tears before they can get away. It wouldn't be this way if my dad were here. The last time he came home, it was from Alaska. We had grilled cheese sandwiches in the middle of the night, and my dad told us all about the bears he'd gone to photograph. My mom said, "There's school tomorrow."

Dad swirled her around the room. "And there's life right now." He kissed the side of her neck under her ear. "I missed you both so much!"

She had to smile. He made everyone smile. Even Claire. It wouldn't be like this if he were here.

Mom turns off the lamp and sits there in the dark. I know I should go to her, but I don't. I can't. I creep carefully back up the stairs.

Standing in the dark in the upstairs hallway, I hear it. Someone crying. *Claire crying?*

I don't know what to do. I stand there in the dark in the middle of the hallway for what seems like a long time. Then I go back to my own room and close the door.

eight

The morning is cloudy and dull. I drink two glasses of orange juice and manage to get half a blueberry muffin down. I wonder who made the muffins. They're good. Or they would be if I cared how things taste.

I'm just finishing when Mom comes into the kitchen. The dark circles under her eyes look like bruises.

"Morning," she says. She opens the freezer door and roots around, pulling out a brick of coffee. I watch her start the coffeemaker, but I don't say anything. She sits across from me, puts a muffin on her plate and then ignores it.

"I'm going out to rake leaves," I tell her. I know I'm a coward, leaving her to deal with Claire alone after last night.

"You don't have to do that, D'Arcy. I thought I'd hire someone."

"I can do it. I want to. Really." I'm chicken.

She opens her mouth and then closes it with a sigh. "All right. Whatever you want."

"Anything you need before I go out?"

She shakes her head.

I get my jacket and look in the closet for a pair of gloves. As I pass the table again, something makes me put my hand on Mom's shoulder for a moment. I hear a catch in her throat as she takes a breath.

"Sure you don't need anything?" I ask as I push by.

Her eyes are shiny. "I'm just fine," she says. "Go on."

*
**

Two big bags of leaves later, I see Claire coming across the grass toward me, hands jammed into the pockets of her trench coat. This is my sister. This is the only other person who is connected to my dad in the same way that I am. But I don't feel connected to her.

"Hi," Claire says as she reaches me.

"Hi." I keep on raking. The teeth of the rake make a metallic swish as they scrape the ground.

"I just came to tell you that I'm ready to leave."

"Have a good trip." I'm watching her sideways, studying her face. Are her eyes puffy?

Do it, the voice in my head insists. The words fall out of my mouth before I have any more time to think about them. "I think it was an accident."

Claire closes her eyes for a moment. "It wasn't."

"You don't know that," I say.

"I know you don't want to believe it, but he killed himself, D'Arcy. He didn't want to be"—her jaw moves like she's testing the feel of some word before she says it—"here anymore."

"No," I say, staring down at the ground. I've raked the same piece of grass so much there aren't any leaves left. The rake is flinging up bits of dirt.

"Pretending isn't going to change it."

I stop, lean on the rake and look at her full on. "I'm not pretending. You don't know that he…" I can't get the words to come out of my mouth. I try again. "You don't know that he didn't have an accident. Nobody knows. The police aren't done. Why don't you just believe in him, Claire?"

She looks out across the yard, at the trees, the rock wall, the empty flowerbeds. Finally she looks back at me. "I'm sorry," she says, so quietly I'm not quite sure she spoke.

We stand there for two breaths.

"I better get going then." We both hesitate, eyeing the couple of feet between us as though it were a trench filled with crocodiles. For a moment it feels as though we're moving toward each other too slowly even for it to be seen. Then the moment passes. I wrap both hands around the rake handle.

"Good-bye, Claire," I say.

"Good-bye."

She turns and heads back across the lawn. I remember the sound of her crying. *Go after her*, the voice in my head says. *At least give her a hug. She's your sister.* I take one step. And then I remember all the things she said to my mother

34

last night. If there's any part of my father in her, I can't find it. I can't do it. I can't hug Claire. I don't know which bothers me more, hugging Claire or finding out whether she'd hug me back.

*
**

The house is quiet. Now and then I hear a car pass on the street. Not very often though. It's Saturday, almost Sunday.

I'm lying in bed on my stomach, the pillows wedged under my shoulders so I can see my clock. I watch the little red bars change: 55...56...57...58...I'm waiting for the week to be over.

I want my life to be normal again. I want the dead empty place inside me to disappear.

I want my dad.

nine

"You should go back to school," Mom says. She's wearing the plaid robe and a pair of my dad's wool socks instead of slippers.

"You aren't going back to work," I counter. We're at the kitchen table, Mom hanging over a cup of coffee, me with a bowl of half-eaten, soggy cereal in front of me. I'm not sure how it suddenly got to be Monday morning, but it is.

"I have some things to take care of."

"I'll help."

She shakes her head. "I don't want you to miss any more time. Exams aren't that far away."

The phone rings. For a second I freeze. It's not even seven o'clock. My heart is pounding in my ears. Then I remember. How bad could it be? The worst has already happened.

I reach for the phone. Am I ever going to stop jumping when it rings this early in the morning? "Hello?"

"Hey. It's just me."

Brendan. I breathe again. "Hi." I mouth his name at Mom.

"I just called to see if you're okay and if you're going to school."

"I don't know. Maybe. I mean about the school part."

"I could skip practice and drive you." Brendan is on the basketball team.

"No. I'm not sure yet. Go."

"If you need me to—"

"I'm fine. Go."

"Are you sure?"

"Yes." I sound mad, I realize. I don't mean to.

"Okay. Am I going to see you tonight?"

I toss a quick glance at my mom. There are some things I need to do. "Maybe. I'll call you."

"Are you sure you're all right?"

Why is he being like this? "Yes. My cereal's getting soggy though."

"Sorry. I'll talk to you later."

I hang up.

Mom looks at me. "D'Arcy. Go to school. There's nothing you can do here."

Suddenly I want to get out. "All right," I say.

I get dressed, brush my teeth, throw my books into my backpack. It doesn't take very long.

"I don't know if I'll be here when you get home," Mom says. "But I shouldn't be too late."

"Okay."

"Then I'll see you whenever."

"Okay." I feel like I'm six years old and it's the first day of school. My breakfast sloshes around in my stomach. I make myself pull on my jacket and go out the door.

I walk quickly, my breath hanging for a moment in front of my face and then thinning into nothing in the cold morning air. I like walking. It's good for thinking. Or for not thinking.

The morning smells like car exhaust. Dad wanted to move out of the city, where it was cleaner. He always said that breathing this air was going to be the death of us all.

Not now. Not all of us.

I take the bottom part of the hill in long strides and turn down Duke Street toward the school. The sun's high and bright but it has no warmth. The school's just in front of me, past the next corner, when my feet suddenly stop.

I look across at the old stone building with the heavy wooden doors and old drafty windows. It feels like a million years since I was last inside.

I put out my hand and touch the trunk of a tree. They're all along the street. They're older than the school. I rub my hand back and forth on the scratchy bark, scraping my skin.

How can I do it? How can I go in there and see people and talk to them? What if, somehow, people know? They're going to say stupid things, wrong things. I don't know what to say back.

There's a sour lump at the back of my throat that I can't swallow down. Okay, five minutes. I'll try it for five minutes but that's it.

I head down the sidewalk toward the main doors just like everyone else. I just want it to be normal. Can't one part of my life be normal again?

ten

Seth Thomas stops me at the stairs. He's the peer tutor in my advanced math class. Peer tutor is what they do with kids who are smarter than the teachers. He's my age and he's doing college-level calculus.

"D'Arcy, I heard about your dad. I'm sorry," Seth says. He doesn't wait for me to say anything, doesn't seem to expect me to. He hands me a bunch of papers. "These are all the notes of what you missed, and you don't have to worry about the assignment."

I nod.

Seth swings his leather pack onto one shoulder and shoves his hair out of his face. "That's my e-mail on the top page. In case...you know, you have any problems."

"Umm, thanks," I say.

"No problem," he says and disappears down the stairs.

I hold the pages tightly. This I can figure out. There's

only one answer to these problems, and the answers always make sense.

Marissa is leaning on my locker in jeans and her suede jacket with the fringe. She has all these great clothes because her mother is a buyer for Willington's department store—not just the store here, but all the stores in this part of the country. And she gets to travel with her mom a lot. She's been to New York twice, and last year she went to Paris for five days.

"Hi," she says. "I wasn't sure you'd be here today."

"I didn't think *you* would," I say as I work the combination of my lock. Marissa has been out of school for almost two weeks with some weird flu.

"I got sick of being home. After *The Young and the Restless*, there's not much to do." She frowns. I can feel her studying my face while I stow my jacket and search for books. "What about you? You okay?"

Here it comes. "I'm all right."

"I really wanted to come to the funeral, but I had this freaky cough. I sounded like a seal."

"It's okay, about the funeral," I say. "I got your note."

Marissa stares down at her feet. "I...uh...want you to know that I'm sorry. I really liked your dad. He was fun. Not like my dad." She looks up at me and makes a face. "Do this. Don't do that. Mostly don't do that. It's all my dad knows how to say."

I keep my head inside my locker, moving books around so I don't have to talk.

She snaps one purple fingernail with the other. "D'Arcy, you'd call me if you wanted to talk, right?"

"Sure," I mumble.

"Even if it's the middle of the night, you can call me."

I turn to look at her. "Yeah, I know."

"You can tell me anything," she says.

What is the matter with her? She has this look on her face like she's wearing a thong that's too small. This is what I didn't want: people acting all weird. I slam my locker door and snap the lock.

We head down the hall to homeroom. Marissa's walking backward. "Hey," she says, "do you remember the time your dad came back from Mexico, and he got us out of study hall and we went out and had burritos? He had that big sombrero on and it was sticking out of the sunroof." She laughs. "Your dad was so cool."

I nod. I remember. I just don't want to.

Before we go into class, Marissa grabs my arm. "Listen. If you just can't stand sitting in there, pull on your hair or something. I can still do the cough, and it's like I'm gonna pass out." She snaps her fingers. "And just like that we're off to the nurse's office."

"That's so sneaky," I say.

"But effective." She grins, and I almost manage a grin back.

*
**

It's getting dark when I get home. That's the thing I hate most about this time of year, more than the cold. I feel as though all my life outside of school is happening in the dark.

There aren't any lights on in the house. "Mom?" I call.

No answer. The car's in the driveway. Where is she? I feel that stomach-falling, top-of-the-roller-coaster sensation inside.

"Mom?"

Nothing.

Some sense, some kind of radar maybe, makes me turn toward the living room. She's there, standing by the window in the almost darkness, as if she and the room were in another place. I touch her arm. "Mom?"

"Beautiful, isn't it, D'Arcy," she says, staring out the window.

"What?"

"The sunset. It was your father's favorite time of day. You know that."

I don't know that. I hear it again, just like this morning when the phone rang so early: my own heartbeat pounding in my ears. I wait until I realize she isn't going to say any more. She just stands there looking out into the night. The first stars are winking on.

"C'mon, Mom," I say at last. "Let's get some supper."

She looks at me. For a moment, less than that really, it seems as though there's no one behind her eyes, just blankness. Then it passes. "Supper? I didn't even think about supper. How about spaghetti?"

"Sounds great," I say.

**

Brendan puts his arm around me, tucks my body close against his. "I'm glad we came," he says, leaning close to my face.

"Yeah," I say, nodding in case he didn't hear me over the music and the people.

We're at the South End Street Fair, which isn't actually on the street at all. It's in an old warehouse close to the waterfront. There are dozens of things to do and see and hear. Lots of sound and color and light and people. It's almost impossible to talk or even think, which is good because I don't want to do either one. It's taken so much energy all week just to act normal. I haven't told Brendan or Marissa or anyone that my dad might have…because we don't know yet. We don't.

"What do you want to do first?" Brendan's breath is warm on my ear.

"I don't care." I have to shout for him to hear me as we get swallowed into the action.

I let him pull me from booth to booth, past painted silk scarves, fat teddy bears in lace collars, and the softest angora sweaters made with the fur of real angora goats—which are also for sale at the same stall. We stop for a while to watch two mimes and again to listen to a couple of musicians, one with a flute and the other on guitar. The tune is fast, happy like laughter, the flute and guitar notes chasing each other.

I try on a beaded denim jacket at one stall. "D'Arcy! Hi." Someone grabs my arm. Marissa. She's wearing a psychedelic bodysuit, all swirling green and orange, with her black leather jacket.

"That looks great on you," she says, looking at the jacket. I flip the tag so she can see the price. "Wow! Are they kidding?"

"I don't think so," I say. I put the jacket back on its hanger.

"I like that one," Marissa says, pointing to a design done with lots of dark beads. "I can just see my dad if I spent that much money for a jacket. He'd start squeezing the sides of his head between his thumb and fingers, and he'd say, 'What does a stroke feel like?'"

She half turns and smiles at the very tall guy behind her, who smiles at me. He has long blond hair in a ponytail and tiny black-framed glasses. "D'Arcy, this is Zack."

"Hi, Zack," I say. Did Marissa tell me about Zack? I don't remember.

"Hi, D'Arcy."

I like his smile and the way all the lines in his face go up.

"Did you try any of the food yet?" Marissa asks.

"We haven't been here that long."

"You have to try the smoked sausage. It's in this big bun with tons of onions and stuff." She looks around and then confides, "I ate a huge one."

Behind her, Zack holds up two fingers.

"And there's this place with apple fritters. Yum." She squeezes her eyes shut with pleasure, then opens them, shaking her head. "God, I'm a pig. I'm so fat."

She slaps her thighs with her palms. Nothing moves. She isn't fat anywhere.

People are pushing past, bumping into us. "We've gotta keep moving," Marissa says. "Some people are so ignorant. See ya."

Zack smiles at me as she pulls him away.

Maybe I'm trying too hard. Maybe it's enough if I just show up and try to look normal.

Brendan comes up behind me and slips his arms around mine. "I'm starved. Wanna eat?"

"Umm, okay."

We make a circuit of all the food stands. I get spring rolls from Betty Fong's, and Brendan decides on the smoked sausage Marissa was going on about, piled high with onions and sauerkraut.

"I'm not sitting next to you and that," I tell him as we snag an empty table. I pull my chair around so we're opposite each other.

"C'mon. How about a little kiss?" he teases, leaning across the table. "You're not afraid of a little puppy breath, are you?"

I bop him on the nose with one of my spring rolls. "No dog with half a nose would go near that thing."

Brendan drops back into his seat laughing. "You know the first time I ever ate one of these? It was the first time I was ever here. Me and you, your mom and dad. Your father said, 'You like sauerkraut?' I said, 'Sure.' I wasn't even sure what sauerkraut was."

He takes another huge bite and starts talking again before he's swallowed it all. "Your dad could eat anything. Remember when we went to Spruce Point? He ate all those corn dogs, and then he got on The Plume and it didn't bother him a bit."

"I remember." I put down my half-finished roll. I'm not as hungry as I thought I was.

"We were all green, holding our stomachs and he goes and gets—"

46

"I remember." I fling out my arms. "I remember. Okay?"

"What's your problem?"

"I don't have a problem. You have a problem." I pull strings of cabbage out of my spring roll. "You don't listen. I told you I remember and you just go on talking."

Brendan jams the end of his sandwich into his mouth, chews it maybe twice and swallows. "What? Is it that time of the month already?" he asks.

I jump up. My chair tips over, hitting the concrete floor with a bang that gets swallowed by the crowd noise. "Shut up," I yell at him. I shove my way through the crowd until I can't see the table anymore. Both of my hands are twisted into fists. If I had any fingernails, they would have poked right into my palms. All of a sudden I want to go home. There's too much noise; too much everything.

Off to one side, people are laughing, pointing. I see a juggler on a unicycle, weaving around the tables and the people. As he gets closer, I see that it's apples he's juggling, circling so fast I can't count how many there really are.

How does he do that?

The juggler stops right in front of me. He is young and thin, with white face paint and shaggy reddish hair. His feet rock on the pedals and somehow he stays upright and in place. I'm mesmerized by all that motion. I think maybe it's what the inside of my head is like. The juggler grins at me. Suddenly his hand goes up, and he flips his top hat into the moving circle and back onto his head again. Then he twists his wrist somehow, and all at once I'm holding a shiny red apple.

We've drawn a crowd. They clap and laugh. The juggler tips his head at the applause and gives me a sideways wink before he moves away.

I get a shivery feeling like someone ran a finger up the back of my neck. I turn around and there is Seth Thomas, just a few feet away, still and quiet as people push by him. When he sees me looking at him, he walks over.

"Hi," he says.

"Hi."

"Did you get caught up on all that math okay?"

"Yeah."

We stare at the people swirling all around us. I don't have anything else to say, and I guess neither does he.

"He's pretty good," Seth says then.

"What?" I say.

He gestures at the apple I'm still holding on to. "The guy who was juggling and riding the unicycle."

"I couldn't do it, that's for sure."

"You could juggle. That's easy."

I shake my head. "I don't think so. He must have had five apples going around. I think about trying to do that… no way."

"So maybe you couldn't do five, but you could keep, say, three balls going." Seth pushes the hair back from his face. I notice he has very long fingers.

"You can juggle?" I say.

"Uh-huh. My…" He stops for a second. "I haven't been doing it that long," he says. He runs his thumb back and forth over the ends of his fingers. "You don't think about it. You just kinda shut off your mind and do it." He shrugs. "I could show you how sometime."

I wonder if he could show me how to shut my mind off, but I don't say it.

Seth looks at me and I get that shivery feeling again, as if somehow he knows how much work it is to act normal. But how could he? "So, I'll see you," he says.

I nod.

I watch him walk away and wonder why it seems he knows things about me that there's no way he can know.

*
**

"Mmmm. It smells good in here," Mom says as she comes through the door.

"Baked potatoes, hamburger casserole and string beans," I tell her, waving my oven mitts at the stove with a flourish. The kind of meal a real family would eat. We can be a family. A normal family, just the two of us. We can do this.

"I don't believe you did all this. I couldn't even remember whether I'd taken anything out of the freezer or not."

"You didn't. But it didn't matter. I nuked the hamburger to thaw it. I think it's all ready if you want to eat."

"It all looks so good and it smells terrific, but I'm really not hungry. I'm sorry, D'Arcy. I'm just too tired to eat."

"I could make you something else," I say. "What about toast and tea?"

She rubs the back of her neck. "Thanks. But I think what I really need is just to soak in a hot tub and go to bed."

"That's all right. I'll just save this, and we'll have it tomorrow."

"Sure. Good night then."

I watch her head upstairs. She did look tired. Really she did.

I fill a plate and take it into the living room. I switch through all the TV channels until I find something with a family in it. And then I sit back and eat my supper.

Sometimes I think we don't exist—Mom and I. I wonder where everyone went. Dad would decide on Saturday morning to have people for dinner, and in a few hours he'd be at the stove making paella, and there would be candles glowing everywhere and exotic drum music coming from the stereo that seemed to make everyone's heart beat faster. I don't know what happened to all those people who laughed and talked and ate in this house. Do they think death is like a disease they could catch just from being in the same room with us?

eleven

Monday morning as I come down the hill toward the school, I see Seth sitting on the low brick wall that wraps around the old part of the school. He sort of smiles when he sees me. Is he waiting for me? My feet start walking over, and I make myself keep going because it's the normal thing to do, even though I meant to duck inside the bottom door and hide out in the girls' bathroom until the first bell.

"I've got the list of extra-credit problems if you want to look at it," Seth says, holding out some papers. He has blue eyes, I realize. It's the first time I've ever looked close enough at Seth to notice his eyes.

"Oh, thanks," I say. I don't even look at the work; I just jam it in my backpack.

"And these are for you." He's holding out what looks like two purple tea bags.

"What are those things for?" I say. "Are we supposed to figure out their volume or their surface area or something?"

Seth makes a face and grins at me. I think he's the only person at school who talks to my face and not some spot just past my right ear. Everyone else is all awkward and jumpy, almost like they're afraid of me. Like I have the smell of death on me and they might get it on them.

"No, they're for juggling. I thought maybe you'd like to try it."

"No, no, no." I shake my head at him. "I can't do stuff like that."

"Yeah, you can. Watch me." He slides down off the wall and holds one of the tea-bag things in each hand. "Look, it's easy," he says. "Toss the beanbag in your right hand up and over into your left hand."

"Uh, that's not juggling," I say. "That's throwing. I can do that."

I set my backpack on the wall and sit beside it.

"Exactly," Seth says. "That's all juggling is, throwing things from one hand to the other. This time, when this bag starts heading down to my left hand, I'm going to throw the one in that hand over to my right hand." And that's what he does. It looks easy.

"Here, try it," he says, putting the two beanbags back in my hand.

The first bag makes a perfect arc in the air, but I'm still holding the other one. What do I do?

"Help!" I toss the bag at Seth. He catches it. I can see he's trying not to laugh.

"Go ahead and laugh," I say. "I told you I can't juggle."

"You didn't drop anything. That was good."

"Show me again," I say, flipping the second bag over to him.

He shakes his hair out of his face and starts tossing the beanbags back and forth from hand to hand. I try to watch both of his hands at the same time, but it gets too confusing.

"Spectacular finish coming," Seth says. The bags arc twice as high this time. He catches them both and bows.

I clap wildly.

Seth's face gets red. He holds out the purple beanbags. "Here," he says. "Just practice throwing one from your right hand to your left hand."

I stuff them in the pocket of my fleece jacket. "I don't know about this," I say. "I'm not coordinated. I'm not athletic. The first time we played baseball in gym in grade nine I hit the ball right over the fence."

"That was a home run, D'Arcy. That's good."

"Miss Bell yelled run. Everyone on my team yelled run. So I did. The wrong way around the bases."

"No way."

"Uh-huh." I pull my pack onto one shoulder. "I still think it should have counted."

"Juggling is easier," Seth says, grabbing his own backpack off the ledge. "Can you make toast? Can you tie your shoes?"

"Yeah." Somehow we start walking for the door, side by side.

"Then you can learn to juggle."

I give him a *yeah right* look.

"One bag, right to left. Just try it."

"Okay, okay, okay." I hold up my hands like I'm about to surrender. "It can't be any worse than baseball was."

We stop at the stairs just inside the building. I'm going up. Seth is going down. "I'll see you in math then," he says.

Before I can say anything, the bell rings. Seth is swallowed up by the push of kids through the door, and I get swept up the stairs.

⁎

"Why am I taking history?" Marissa asks as we head down the main stairs after our last class.

"Because it's a required course," I tell her. "Besides, you know how much you love listening to Mr. Bailey talk about life in the Middle Ages."

Marissa crosses her eyes at me. "Yeah, isn't that when he was a teenager?" she says. "Hey, look." She points toward our lockers. "Stud Puppy's waiting for you."

Brendan is leaning on my locker. Marissa always calls him Stud Puppy. She says he's about as smart as a big dog. "Hi," I say as we get level with him.

"Hi, big guy," Marissa says, reaching up to mess his hair. I shoot her a warning look, but Brendan doesn't care that she's making fun of him.

"Why aren't you at practice?" I say.

"Cancelled. They're doing something to the floor in the gym, and the track's too wet outside. So I can drive you home." He looks at Marissa. "You want a ride?"

"I already have one," she says, wiggling her eyebrows, which I think is supposed to look sexy. She shoves books into her locker, pulls others out and finally grabs her jacket. "Call me later," she says over her shoulder as she walks away.

I grab my own stuff and pull on my jacket. Brendan slips his arm around me as we head down the hall, turning my face against his shoulder. He leans down and tickles my ear with his tongue.

"Hey, stop that," I say. "You're going to get us caught."

Mr. Connell, the vice-principal, doesn't approve of PDAs in the halls. That's what he calls public displays of affection.

"There's no one around," Brendan says. He doesn't worry about things like that. He's Mr. Hotshot Basketball Star, so the rules aren't quite the same for him.

In the car I let Brendan talk, and the words just slide all around me. I hear maybe every fifth or sixth one. As we turn onto my street, I catch a whole sentence.

"...don't have to be there until six. So we have a couple of hours all to ourselves." Before I can say anything, he swings into the driveway. "Shit!" he exclaims.

My mom's car is in front of the garage. I let out the breath that I didn't realize I was holding. "There's still a lot of paper-work," I say. "She doesn't stay at work the whole day."

"I never see you," Brendan says. I know that's not exactly what he means.

"I'm sorry," I say. "I better go in. I'll call you later."

"Okay."

"I'm sorry," I say again as I get out of the car. But as I watch him drive away, all I feel is relief.

*
**

I'm coming from the bathroom, my wet hair cold on the back of my neck. My eyes slide past the half-open bedroom door without really looking, and I take two or three more steps before it registers that something's different.

I back up, nudge the door all the way open with my foot. The quilt is gone from the bed, all those different shades of green replaced by a dull gray polar fleece blanket. The quilt had been an anniversary present for my mother. I remember my dad telling us about the old ladies who had done the quilting. One of them had been a hundred and one and had flirted like crazy with him.

Where is it? Where did she put it?

I haven't been inside my parents' room—my mother's room—since it happened. I take a step across the floor. Then another.

It isn't right. My dad's clothes should be falling off the chair in the corner by the window. His comb and his watch should be on the dresser. Why aren't his shoes in the middle of the floor, like he just stepped out of them and kept walking? Where's the stack of books next to his side of the bed?

I'm breathing very fast but I can't seem to get any air. I jam my knuckles in my mouth and bite until it hurts. I bite until I can breathe right again.

My father's dresser is empty. I yank out every drawer but nothing of his is left behind. I jerk the closet doors open. Mom's clothes are hanging on one side but the other side is empty. Not even a hanger.

Where is everything? When did she do this?

There is nothing of my father's left in this room. His shoes are gone from the closet floor. The hat with the earflaps he brought back from Alaska is missing from the shelf. And his Indiana Jones hat is gone too.

Why? Why?

I sit in the closet, my back against the wall. If she really loved him, how could she pack up all his things just like that? I feel as though someone's fist is jammed up inside my chest. It's hard to breathe. It's hard to swallow. I don't even know I'm crying until the tears drip onto my hands.

I wait until after supper the next night to ask my mother about Dad's things. We're in the kitchen. Mom is putting stuff in the fridge, and I'm flattening the pizza box.

"What did you do with Dad's stuff?" I ask.

Her back's turned. She stiffens and pulls her arms in against her body. She doesn't turn around. "What do you mean?"

"I mean his clothes, his books, everything. Where is it?" I smash the corners of the box lid flat.

I'm waiting for her to ask me how I know it's all gone, but she doesn't. She straightens up and turns to face me.

"I gave his clothes to the Salvation Army and his books and other things to the shelter."

"So some old drunk on the street is walking around puking on Dad's clothes?" My hands are twisting the cardboard lid, crushing it. I drop it on the floor.

"I gave your father's things to people who could use them." She speaks slowly like I've suddenly gone stupid.

"You threw them away!" The words burst out.

She flinches and closes her eyes for a second. "None of those things were doing any good here."

"You don't even care. You want to make it look like he was never here," I shout. "Are you going to take me to the Salvation Army next, Mom?"

"Don't do this," Mom says, shaking her head. Her whole body sags. The refrigerator door hangs open.

"Why? You keep doing things and you don't even ask me."

"None of it was good for anything."

"You didn't even ask me!" I scream the words.

I don't want to be in the same room as her anymore. As I shove past her, my elbow bangs the refrigerator door. The bottles inside rattle like chattering teeth. I kick the door, putting all my anger into it. The door bangs shut, and I am out of the room. Behind me I hear my mother calling my name, but I don't answer.

twelve

We're working on quadratic equations in groups of three or four with our desks pulled together when Ms. Henry from the office comes to the classroom door. "D'Arcy, you're wanted in the office," Mr. Kelly says from the doorway.

I stand up and try to swallow past the huge lump that's suddenly in my throat. Ms. Henry says something else to him. He nods and closes the door. "Take your things," he says to me.

I fumble with my notebook, trying to get it closed. My pencil hits the floor and rolls away. Seth snags it with his foot. I jam my stuff into my backpack and head for the door. It seems to get farther away every step I take. Everyone's looking at me.

The hallway's deserted. I start down the stairs to the main floor. My mind is jumping all over the place—anything to avoid thinking about what's going to happen when I get to the office. I can see my mother talking to Mr. Connell as I get to the bottom step, and I have to grab the banister because suddenly I have spaghetti knees. She turns, sees me and turns back to Mr. Connell to offer her hand.

I stay where I am, clutching the railing with one hand and my backpack with the other, until she walks over to me. "Get whatever books you need," she says. "We have to go home."

"What happened?" I ask.

"We'll talk about it when we get home."

"Tell me now."

She shakes her head and doesn't look at me. "When we get home."

We don't talk in the car. I wrap my arms around my backpack. I don't know what's wrong, so I make a list in my head of what I know it can't be. No one else I care about is dead. The house hasn't burned down. I don't have a terminal disease. Then I remember a joke my dad liked to tell. What happens when you play a country song backwards? Your wife comes back. Your dog's alive. And your truck works.

As soon as I'm inside the door, I drop my stuff and turn to her. "Okay, what is it?"

She takes off her jacket. "Come sit down."

"No," I say. "You're stalling. Whatever it is, tell me or I'm going back to school." I back up to the door.

"All right." She's still looking everywhere but at me. "The police have officially...they're ruling your father's death a suicide."

The room begins to spin around me. I slide down the door until I hit the floor. "All because the car went off the road?

That doesn't mean anything." My voice sounds garbled, like I'm talking underwater.

"It's more than that."

"What?"

She shakes her head.

"Tell me."

She stays silent.

"Fine. I'll go to the police station and someone there will tell me." But I don't get up because I can't.

"He wasn't himself," Mom whispers.

"Tell me," I say louder.

"He'd been drinking. There weren't any skid...the mark from...from the gas pedal was...his shoe...he didn't have his seat belt on."

"No. He didn't...he didn't drive into the river on purpose. People who do...who do that, they're depressed. He was fine. He was happy."

She reaches for me. I jerk away and bolt for the den. There are papers on the desk—bills and cards left over from the funeral. I sweep them all onto the floor. "D'Arcy, what the hell are you doing?" Mom is in the doorway.

"People that...they leave notes. If he did that, where's the note?"

Mom closes her eyes for a second. "Not always," she says softly.

I'm breathing fast and hard and it's making me dizzy. I grab a desk drawer, drop a handful of pens onto the carpet and then dump the drawer on the floor. "There's nothing here. You see? Nothing."

I pull out another drawer, push pens and post-its around and then drop it too.

"D'Arcy, stop. There's nothing here," Mom says.

"That's what I'm trying to tell you." I'm shouting now. "There's nothing because you're wrong." I open the cupboard under the window where she keeps paper and envelopes and a roll of Bubble Wrap. I yank the shelf inside off the little plastic pins, and everything spills down onto the floor.

Mom tries to reach for me but I pull away and push past her.

I have to show her. Where? The living room? The dining room? My dad's books fill up most of the shelves on one whole wall in the living room. I grab a big hardcover book from the middle shelf, hold on to the front and back covers and shake. "Look," I shout. "Nothing." I drop it and pull another down. "Nothing." Then another.

Behind me I hear my mother yelling, "D'Arcy! Stop it. Stop it!"

I start to hum, as loud as I can, to drown her out. I have to show her she's wrong.

A small, brown pottery pig that my dad brought back from Mexico squats in the center of the shelf. With one long sweep I shove the rest of the books onto the floor. My mother grabs one of my arms from behind.

The pig smashes into dozens of pieces on the hardwood floor, all except for one pointed shard that flies up and sticks in the side of my free hand. I hold out my arm, watch the blood well up and trickle down around my wrist. But I don't feel anything.

I hear my mother's voice and the sound of bits of pottery crunching under my feet as she pulls me away, down onto my knees. Mom squats beside me and tries to put her arms around me. I twist away and curl into a tight ball. The only sound I hear is my breathing as the tears slide down my face and drip onto my hand.

But I don't feel anything.

*
**

It takes four stitches to close the gash in the side of my hand. A nurse gives me a needle in my hip that makes me feel slow and fuzzy. An intern who smells like pizza and doesn't look any older than me does the stitching. I guess the cut isn't bad enough for me to get a real doctor.

I wonder if this is where they brought my dad after the accident. Did he get a real doctor or just some guy with hair flopping in his eyes and pepperoni breath?

The nurse gives my mother a little tube of cream and instructions about changing the bandage around my hand, like I'm too stupid to do it myself. I don't even look at them. Instead I stare at a poster on the wall about the misuse of antibiotics. Finally Mom says, "Okay, we can go."

She doesn't even try to talk to me on the way home. I stare silently out the passenger window. A couple of times I glance at my mother out of the corner of my eye, but she never looks away from the road. Finally she pulls into the driveway and shuts off the car. I hear her shift in her seat.

Don't touch me.

She clears her throat. "D'Arcy, I know how you feel," she says.

No, you don't, because I don't feel anything.

"Your father wasn't thinking clearly. Because he never would have…" She clears her throat again. "He loved you very much. More than anything in the world."

In my mind I turn down the volume so her voice sounds like it's coming through the radio from a station hundreds of miles away. I'm not listening. I don't hear anything. I just stare out the car window. After a minute my mother gets out of the car. I stay, stiff and still, in my seat.

I don't hear anything.

I don't feel anything.

thirteen

The den looks like a hurricane's blown through it. I've seen rooms, houses, that look like this on the news after a storm. I step over the stuff on the floor, find one of the drawers and slide it back into the desk. I don't know what to do next.

I drop into the chair. I can hear my mother in the living room, putting books back on the bookshelf. She's wrong. I know she is. I knew my father better than anyone.

A wadded-up ball of paper sits in the middle of the broken shelf from the cupboard.

For a moment I forget how to breathe. Then somehow I suck in air with a gurgle that sounds like I'm choking. I slide out of the chair onto my knees. A wadded-up ball of paper... with my father's writing on it.

No.

My hand reaches out and jerks back. I try again and pick it up this time: a couple of sheets of ripped-up, crumpled white paper, covered with my dad's sharp-edged writing. My fingers shake so much the paper falls to the floor.

"Mom," I croak. My breath starts coming faster because, Oh my God, oh God, I know what it is. My hands are scrambling to smooth out the pieces, and I hear my voice screaming for my mother as though it's someone else's. And then she's behind me. "Daddy," I manage to choke out, but she's seen the jagged words on the scraps of paper.

"No," she whispers, closing her eyes for less than a second. She pushes me into the chair. "I'm going to do it, baby. Sit. Sit."

My knees buckle. Every part of me is shaking now. Mom kneels, pulls apart the last of the wadded paper and begins fitting the pieces together like a jigsaw puzzle. She fumbles around on the floor and grabs half a roll of duct tape. Tearing pieces of tape with her teeth, she fits the bits of paper together.

I am so cold, and I feel as though I'm sliding down, down into a dark tight tunnel. Mom's repeating something, almost under her breath. My father's name: David, David, David, David.

"It doesn't make any sense," she says, smoothing the paper flat. I don't have any answer. I don't think she's looking for one. I can't even make out most of the words on the patched pages, the writing is all scratchy lines. Only one scrawl of letters near the bottom even looks like a word—*Nothing*. It doesn't make any sense. It's too cold, and I'm too tired.

I hear Mom say my name as though she were a long way away. She peels off her sweater and pulls it over my head without even slipping my arms through the armholes.

Then she pushes into the chair beside me and pulls me into her lap. "It's okay," she says, stroking my hair.

I pull my arms in against my chest under her sweater and let my mother's warmth soak into me. She turns us in the chair and pulls the phone closer. My mind holds pieces of the conversations, lets others go. "...it's an emergency. Find him. Mark—we...David left a note...okay. I can do that." She hangs up and dials again. "Detective Ridley, please. It's Leah Patterson. It's important."

I can only focus on fragments of what comes next. Mark's a lawyer, my dad's friend. He comes. And a police officer. "She needs to go to the hospital," somebody says. But we were already there. Then Mark folds my fingers around a cup. It's warm and smells like chocolate. I take small sips and watch the tropical fish swim across the screen of the computer that no one thought to turn off.

I don't even know I'm crying until Mom wipes my face with the heel of her hand. We're alone. I've lost some chunk of time.

"I don't...understand," I say.

"Neither do I," she says, her voice raspy, like it hurts her throat for the words to come out. "I'm sorry." A tear gets away and runs down her cheek. She leans over the back of the chair and wraps her arms around my shoulders. "I'm sorry, I'm sorry," she says against my hair.

I don't say anything. The fish glide through the make-believe water. *Sorry, sorry, sorry*, echoes inside my brain.

Something cool brushes my cheek. My mother's hand. I smell cherries—that hand lotion she uses.

Where am I? I want a drink. My lips are cracking and stuck to my teeth.

I'm in that place between asleep and awake. I try to open my eyes, make words, but it's so fuzzy and warm and...fuzzy, and I feel myself falling back down...

*
**

My mouth tastes like metal. I licked a penny once, trying to make it spit shiny. The taste in my mouth is like that. Under the gauze my hand throbs like a bass string thrumming. I open my eyes, and for a second the room swirls around the bed. It's like watching the Twirl-a-Whirl at Spruce Point go whipping by.

How did I get here? I don't remember coming up the stairs, taking off my jeans and sweater, finding these pajamas. The last thing I remember is...no...

I clutch my stomach with one hand, roll over and hang my head over the side of the bed. I keep my eyes closed and press the side of my face against the cold metal rail of the bed frame. In my head I can see that wadded-up ball of paper and the almost unreadable words. It doesn't prove anything. I push the back of my hand against my eyes until all I can see is blackness shot with little flashes of light, like a star-filled sky on a moonless night.

I can hear myself breathing, in and out, in and out, fast, like I'm trying to run away from someone. I concentrate on that sound, on each breath, and after a few minutes the room stops spinning and my stomach stops lurching, for the most part.

I sit up. My T-shirt is crumpled and damp and twisted half sideways. One leg of my pajama pants is hiked up past my knee. I push my hair out of my face. It's a frenzy of curls.

Just then the door eases open and my mother looks in. "You're awake. Hi," she says.

She's wearing jeans and a dark green sweater, not work clothes. Is it Saturday? No.

"What...what time is it?" I ask. My voice sounds like I've been shouting too much.

"It's a bit after ten."

"I'm late." I swing my feet over the side of the bed and try to get up, but I can't seem to get my arms and legs to work together.

"Stay there. I already called the school," Mom says.

"Brendan is going to pick me up." I try to lick my lips. They're rough with flakes of chapped skin.

Mom looks away from me. "I told him you're not going to school today." She clears her throat. "I said you had the stomach flu."

"Oh." The room's cold. I pull my knees up to my chest and wrap my arms around them.

"Take your time."

"Umm, all right," I say.

She turns to go, then stops in the doorway. "I'm sorry, D'Arcy," she says.

Her voice is so quiet I have to lean forward to hear her. For a second it feels as though the walls are coming in at me. I grab the mattress with both hands and the feeling passes as quickly as it came.

Mom still has her back to me. One hand grips the doorknob. The other is squeezed into a fist. "I'm sorry you had to find that…note. I'm sorry your father…did…what…he did."

"What do you mean? You really think he…? Because of some torn-up paper?"

She turns back around. "D'Arcy, honey," she starts, but I cut her off.

"It doesn't mean anything." I shake my head, keep shaking it like a little kid would. "He didn't. It was an accident."

"Your father was sick." She says each word carefully, like I'm too stupid to know what she means.

"You mean crazy? You think he was crazy?" My voice is getting louder.

"No. I found out…" She stops. Takes a couple of breaths. "I talked to the police and the doctor…this morning. He…he had…he had ALS."

"What do you mean? What's ALS?"

Her mouth moves before the words come out. "Amyotrophic lateral sclerosis. Sometimes people call it Lou Gehrig's disease."

"Sclerosis? You mean like multiple sclerosis? Like Brendan's aunt has?"

"No." She keeps running her hands down the sides of her jeans. "ALS is a lot worse."

I pull at the neck of my T-shirt. It's too tight. It's hard to breathe and my voice sounds funny. "What do you mean by worse?" I ask.

"It…people with ALS…their muscles get weaker. They fall, they drop things. Eventually they can't walk or talk. Some can't even breathe without help."

"So what do you do for it? Physio? That's not so bad. Brendan went last year. Remember?" I can't seem to stop talking. "Are there pills? Pills would be better because you know Dad's kind of wussy about needles."

Mom just shakes her head.

"There must be some way to fix it. Right?"

"There's no..." She takes a couple of shaky breaths. "There's no cure for ALS. I don't think he could...live with what was going to happen to him." She takes a couple of steps closer to me and touches my cheek. I twist my head away.

"No. You're wrong." I scramble off the bed, around to the foot, and grab hold of a bedpost. Blood is starting to soak through the bandage on my hand. I stick out an arm to keep her back. "Don't touch me," I warn her. My face is hot and I feel like I'm going to heave. "He would have said if he was sick. The doctor made a mistake, mixed him up with someone else."

"Your dad and Dr. Marshall went to school together. He didn't make a mistake. He's been in Haiti for the last month with Hospitals Without Walls. He didn't even know your father had died."

I get an image of my dad, driving down the road, coming to the turn, hitting the gas, twisting the wheel—No. No. No.

"He wouldn't do something like that," I scream at her. "Maybe, maybe..." I'm shaking. "Maybe he didn't love you enough, but he loved me and he wouldn't...he wouldn't just leave me!"

Her body sags. "He was sick," she says softly. She reaches out as if she's going to touch me, but she doesn't. Her hand hovers in the air for a moment and then drops. "He wasn't—," she begins.

I press both hands over my ears and start to hum the way I did last time she tried to say things I didn't want to hear. Finally she turns and goes out, closing my door behind her. I lie on the bed with my palms tight against my head and keep on humming.

fourteen

When I wake up, it's dark except for a rectangle of light reaching across the floor from the bedroom window. I'm clammy with sweat, and my shirt is sticking to the middle of my back. For a moment I can't figure out what time it is and why I woke up. Then I remember. My father killed himself. It can't be true, but it is.

I'm shaking so hard it feels like the bed is moving. I don't want to go back to sleep. I grab the quilt, wrap it around me and drop into my rocking chair.

Dad found the chair, mostly in pieces, in a corner of the basement. My mother thought it was junk, but he said it had potential. He sanded all the pieces, glued them back together and then painted it a pale, creamy yellow, the color of butter. Only he called it the color of "a heart-healthy, polyunsaturated, trans-fat–free margarine." Even Mom laughed at that.

I don't want to think about that. I don't want to think about my dad at all.

The two little beanbags Seth gave me are on my dresser. I pick one up and toss it from one hand to another. My left hand hurts and there's dried blood on the gauze bandage, but I throw the bag again, and again. I concentrate on throwing the bag in a smooth arc about as high as my eyebrows. And I don't think about anything else.

At all.

*
**

One by one I type the letters, all in caps, into the search engine: *A, L, S*. I click on *Search* and look away quickly. I want to know, and I don't. It's late. The house is dark and silent. Through the window I can see the moon, a thin sliver hanging high in the night sky.

I have to look. Four hundred and nineteen thousand, one hundred and eighty-one hits. I click on the first link and watch the site load.

I don't even know what I'm looking for. An explanation? A reason? Some way of figuring out what was in my father's head, maybe?

...when a person has ALS something goes wrong with the nerves that carry instructions from the brain to the muscles... muscles in the legs, arms and throat....difficulty walking...may need a cane...a wheelchair...difficulty holding things...

It's everything my mother said. His legs would have stopped working. His arms. How could he have taken pictures? How could he have crossed a glacier in a wheel-chair? Or bargained in a market with no voice? How could he have pointed a camera? Or even picked it up? How could he have been himself anymore? Is that what he thought? Is that why he...?

I can't see the screen anymore. I hear someone crying, and I realize it's me.

fifteen

I'm late and my stupid-ass locker won't open. It's Monday and I'm back at school. If I stay away too long, people will start asking questions I don't want to answer right now.

I do the combination again and pull at the lock. It won't open.

I start yanking at it, harder and harder, my fist smashing back against the door. It won't open. It still won't open.

A hand comes over my shoulder and grabs my hand. "What's the combination?"

Seth.

I can feel the heat of his warm hand sinking into my icy one. I pull my hand away and tell him the numbers. He turns the dial slowly, and when he pulls the lock, it lets go.

I start grabbing books.

Seth holds out a bunch of paper. "Here. I hope you're feeling better. This is everything you missed. If it doesn't make sense, let me know." He sets the lock inside my locker and walks away.

"Thanks," I say quietly.

He lifts one arm so I know he heard me, but he doesn't look back.

*
**

I'm running on a gravel path that's hard and lumpy underneath my feet. I stumble over a hollow spot and almost fall. My legs ache and the cold bites my chest with each breath. Silence wraps around me as though I'm the only person in the world.

I'm in the cemetery. Ahead I see what I've been looking for: a stake with a red cardboard tag, lifting on a wisp of wind I can't even feel. It marks the place where the stone will be. I start across the grass to it and remember what my grandmother used to say when she had that goose-bumps-up-the-back, half-déjà vu, half-spooked feeling: Someone just walked over my grave. I veer to the right and try to stay between the markers.

There's a large rectangle of dirt in front of the stake. I squat down and lay my hand on the rough ground. It's so cold. What made me think I would find answers here?

Why didn't he tell us he was sick? How could he not say anything? Did he think I wouldn't love him if I knew? How could he just get in his car and—?

I feel like hitting someone, or smashing something. I want someone else to hurt as much as I do. I need to ask him why he thought that driving into the river was the only thing to do.

I scrape frantically at the ground but my fingers can't dig into the frozen dirt.

I don't know why I came. My dad isn't here.

He isn't anywhere.

*
**

Mom is sitting at the kitchen table reading a magazine. She has one hand snaked around a cup of coffee. She doesn't even pretend that she's drinking herbal tea anymore. The packages are gone. There's a box of coffee filters in their place. She looks up as I walk in and slides a folded piece of paper across the table at me.

"What's this?" I say.

"A note for your teacher so you won't have to spend the rest of the week in detention for cutting your last class yesterday," Mom says. "They called. The school notices things like that."

"It wasn't a class. It was study hall," I say. That much is true. "I felt crappy. I just came home." Eventually.

She looks at me as though she's trying to decide if I'm telling the truth. "D'Arcy, is everything all right?"

"Yeah, I've got cramps, that's all." I slide the note for Mr. Keating off the table and slip it into my pocket. Mom turns back to her magazine.

*
**

"D'Arcy, I'd like to see you for a minute, please," Mr. Keating calls as the bell rings.

Marissa rolls her eyes at me. "Wait for me," I mouth. She nods. I go up to the front while everyone else files out. What does he want? I already gave him the note this morning. My heart is pounding. He can't hear it, can he? No.

I take a couple of deep breaths. Act normal, I tell myself. He doesn't know anything.

Mr. Keating waits until only the two of us are left in the room. Then he leans forward with his elbows on the desk. His tie is pulled to one side, and he has chalk dust on his hands.

"D'Arcy, I just wanted to ask how you're doing," he says.

"All right," I say. What does he want?

"You're caught up on what you missed?"

"I am." Where is this going?

"Good." He tents his dusty fingers together. His long face makes me think of a horse in wire-rimmed glasses. A bald horse.

"I just wanted you to know that if you have any troubling thoughts, if you need to talk to someone, I'm here." He clears his throat. "I know how difficult it must have been to lose your father."

I have a silly urge to say, "But he's not lost. We know exactly where he is." What I do is say, "Thank you, sir. I will."

I won't.

He studies my face as though he's trying to figure out if I'm being straight with him. I give him my half-serious, half-sad, holding-up-nobly face. Then he says, "You can go now."

Out in the hallway, Marissa and Andie are waiting for me.

"Well?" Marissa asks.

"He just wanted to make sure that I was all caught up."

"That's it?"

"That's it." I can fake them out too.

Andie leans against the locker beside mine while I sort my books. She's more Marissa's friend than mine, but she's okay.

"I was at the mall last Friday night. I saw Mr. Keating," she says, fake casual, inspecting the toe of one black lace-up boot.

"Big thrill." Marissa crosses her arms.

"With his girlfriend."

"Girlfriend?" Marissa pounces on the word. "Keating has a girlfriend? No way." She shakes her head so hard her hair bounces.

"How do you know it was his girlfriend?" I ask.

"He had his arm around her, and he wasn't acting like she was his sister."

"So, what's she like?" Marissa asks.

"Well, she had a lot of hair and she was wearing this T-shirt with Mickey Mouse on the front." She holds out her hands, cupped, in front of her. "Mickey's ears were big. Really big."

Marissa gives a snort of laughter.

"And that's not all he has." Andie's lips are twitching at the corners.

"What?" I ask.

"He has a toupee."

"You lie!" Marissa exclaims.

"Swear." Andie puts her hand over her heart. "Looked just like a little curly sheep butt sitting on his head."

At that exact moment, Mr. Keating comes out of the classroom and starts down the hall toward us. Marissa jams her hand in her mouth and keeps her back turned. Andie's face is instantly serious, as though a switch had flipped inside her head.

Mr. Keating nods at us as he passes. He disappears up the stairs and Marissa and Andie explode with laughter, shaking, sputtering, grabbing their stomachs. I make myself laugh too. I catch sight of our reflection in the glass front of a picture of the class of 1976 up on the wall. I look just like they do. I look normal even though I'm not.

sixteen

It was a mistake to come here. I'm standing in the front entrance of the seniors' center. I guess if you're not old, you're pretty much invisible in here, because I've been standing around for about ten minutes and no one's even noticed me.

This was a bad idea. I looked it up online: ALS Support Group. I carried the address around for four days and now it's Wednesday, which is when they have their meeting. And I'm here, but I can't seem to go any farther and I can't seem to leave.

I don't even know why I came except...except I want to see what it looks like when you have ALS. I want to know what about it made my father think being dead was better.

There's a bulletin board on the wall in front of me with colored cardboard strips tacked to it that say what's going on where. A purple strip says there's seniors' tai chi in room 4.

There's a conversational French class in room 12, according to a green strip. And in room 21, ALS Support Group.

I can't do this. What was I thinking? That I could just go in and stare at them like they're some kind of circus. What would I say? "Hi. My dad had what you have so he killed himself, and I just came here to see if it's really that bad."

I turn from the bulletin board and bang into the side of a wheelchair. I grab the back to keep from falling into the lap of the man in the chair. "I'm sorry," I say.

"My fault," he says, smiling up at me. He has blond hair pulled back in a ponytail and kind brown eyes. "I was over the posted speed limit for the hallway." He glances at the bulletin board and then back at me. "Could I help you find something?"

"Umm…" Something catches in my throat and I have to cough before I can answer him. "Uh, no," I say. "I…I'm in the wrong place." I give him a quick smile and start to move past him.

"It's okay to be scared," he says.

"What?" I stop and look back over my shoulder at him.

He's still smiling. "You came for the ALS meeting, the support group, didn't you?"

How did he know?

He dips his head toward the bulletin board as though he knows what I'm thinking. "You had your finger on that strip. It was either the group or seniors' tai chi, and you seem a little young for that."

"I changed…I changed my mind," I say, staring at my shoes because I'm too embarrassed to look at him.

"We don't bite," he says. "Some of us drool sometimes, but that's about it."

They drool? "That's all right," I say. I can feel my face burning.

"That was a joke," he says, looking at me over the top of his glasses. "I guess that career in stand-up isn't going to pan out." He glances down at the wheelchair. "When you're in a wheelchair, can you even be a stand-up comedian?" He shrugs and holds out his hand. "I'm Andrew."

"I'm D'Arcy," I say. We shake hands. Andrew's wearing leather gloves without fingers, and he barely squeezes my hand. His left hand is in a brace.

"Look, why don't you walk down with me," he says. "And if you don't want to stay, you don't have to."

I like his smile. Maybe I could go down the hall with him and—I don't know—just look in the door. That wouldn't be so bad. I nod. "Okay."

Andrew leads the way, steering his chair with what looks like a little joystick. We follow the hall to the end and turn left. Andrew stops at the first door on the right. What looks like an elementary kid's desk, stacked with brochures, is pushed against the door to keep it open.

"You want to come in?" he asks.

There are about a dozen people in the room. Most of them are in wheelchairs like Andrew. There's a woman with a walker and a man with two canes. No one is old. I thought they'd be old.

A woman about my mom's age squats next to a wheel-chair. The man in the chair is typing something on a laptop fastened to his chair. He can use only one finger, and it doesn't always go where he wants it to. I can't stop watching him. Andrew says something else to me, but I don't know what it was. Is this what would have happened to my dad?

The man finishes typing. The woman looks at the screen and starts to laugh, shaking her head. The man's face twists into a grin but no sound comes out of his open mouth. Still laughing, she pulls a Kleenex out of her pocket and wipes the drool off the side of his mouth. And all of a sudden I don't see two strangers. I see my father in that chair and myself crouched on the floor, wiping his chin.

Did he think we wouldn't love him like this? Or...or was it that he didn't love us enough to face the wheelchair and the drooling?

I turn and run for the entrance. I hear Andrew calling my name, but I can't even look at him. I push my way through the people coming up the front steps. Then I'm doubled over at the side of the building next to the sign that says *Redborne Senior Citzens' Center Parking*, palms of my hands jammed against my eyes to shut out the image of the man in the chair, of Dad in that chair.

"I miss you," Brendan says, his mouth on mine. His hand slides under my sweater, moves up my belly. His fingers slither beneath my bra. He makes a sound, almost like a growl in the back of his throat.

I want to squirm out of his arm, out from under his hand.

"I love you," he whispers. "I just want you to feel good."

But I don't. I don't start to breathe faster when he kisses down the curve of my jaw to my mouth. There's no rush of blood thumping in my ears when his tongue tangles with mine. I don't feel anything.

Maybe that doesn't matter. I close my eyes, kiss the curve of his ear and start to slide my hand up his thigh.

But I don't feel anything.

*
**

The movie's already started, but I don't care. I take a seat in the middle, one row from the back, and scrunch down until my knees are pressed against the back of the seat in front of me. There's just enough space for my popcorn between my legs and my chest.

I love the Majestic. Even the name sounds the way a movie theater should, as opposed to Megaplex—twelve theaters, a giant arcade, a food court and thirty-one different popcorn toppings. Stupid.

The Majestic has black velvet curtains that make a rustling sound as they open to show the screen. There are red velour seats with lots of padding that you can squish right down into. The Majestic has real movie food—no nachos with low-sodium salsa. No crudités with fat-free dip. At the Majestic they sell popcorn with real butter and salt, jujubes, cool mints and licorice whips. And the usher wears a drum major's red jacket with lots of braid and a little red hat like an organ-grinder's monkey.

The theater is about half full—mostly students from the university and old people. This is the fourth time I've been here in the middle of the day. I've been faking stomach pains to get out of gym class—I don't want to play badminton or dodgeball. Getting pounded by a big, hard ball isn't fun. It wasn't fun in third grade, and it isn't fun now.

The nurse says my "gastric upset" is caused by stress. She tips her head to one side and pats my arm. Then she gives me two plastic soup spoons of Maalox, reminds me to do the nose breathing she gave me a blue sheet of paper about and signs my library pass. I'm supposed to be studying in the library if I'm not in gym class, but it's easy, I discovered, to sign in and then sneak out. No one ever checks.

The first time I left, I was walking up Duke Street. The whole time I kept expecting Mr. Connell's hand to come from behind me and grab my shoulder. But nothing happened. Not then, not the next day.

That first day I left school I just wandered around the dollar store. The second time, I walked along the street instead of up the hill, and when I got here to the old theater, I bought a ticket and came in without really thinking about it.

The movies are mostly old ones or arty films that the Megaplex would never show because they don't have any car chases or teenagers getting killed by the fat kid they picked on in kindergarten. I don't care what the movies are anyway. In here, for six bucks plus the price of popcorn or some jujubes, I can get away from my life for a few hours.

*
**

Mom is bent over her desk, the heels of her hands pressed to her temples. "Mom," I say softly from the door. I need money.

She drops one hand and looks over her shoulder at me. "I didn't hear you come in," she says.

"How was your meeting?"

She shrugs. "We made a couple of decisions, so I guess it was productive."

Mom is a computer programmer. Mostly she works on programs that do things for doctors and hospitals.

"I didn't mean to interrupt you," I say. "I…uh…I need some money. I need new running shoes for gym and I have to pay the rest of my lab fees." Lab fees were paid in September, and I don't plan on ever going back to gym class. But movies aren't cheap, even in the middle of the day, and I can't exactly tell her what I've been doing. Besides, I like having money in my pocket. It makes me feel like I could go anywhere I want to, do anything I want to.

She reaches for her purse under the desk and counts out four fifty-dollar bills. I jam the money in my back pocket.

"There's something I want to talk to you about," Mom says as she drops her wallet back into her bag. "Sit down for a minute."

"Okay." I pull out one of the dining room chairs and sit, curling my legs under me.

Mom straightens, shrugs her shoulders a couple of times. "I've been thinking about Christmas, D'Arcy."

My dad loved Christmas. I never knew who'd be at the table Christmas Eve when we sat down to supper. He'd invite everyone he'd met all day. "The more the merrier," he'd tell my mom. He'd be cooking in the kitchen and singing Christmas carols. Last year he even got the idea to have a snow angel competition between supper and dessert.

Mom presses her lips together, and I pull my mind back from drifting. "You're almost an adult now," she says. "So I thought I'd just give you money this year."

How much money? I wonder.

"I wouldn't have any idea what to get you. This way you can get whatever you want. And I don't want you spending a lot of money on me. We'll just have a quiet Christmas this year."

It's been decided. It's not like I even want a pile of presents, but she didn't talk to me, she talked at me. "All right," I say. "Whatever you want." Because I don't want to celebrate Christmas anyway.

"Good. I'm glad it's settled." She turns back to her papers.

I grab my coat and slip out the kitchen door. I start walking without any direction in mind. I end up down by the rowing club. Out on the river there's one lone kayaker, slicing through the churning water in an orange shell.

I walk out onto the wooden lookout over the rocks, put my arms up on the railing and look down at the water rushing by, dark and cold, so icy blue that I can't see the bottom. For a moment I wonder what it would be like to climb over the railing, drop down into the cold blue-blackness and let it swirl over my head, to be surrounded by nothing but the rushing sound of the water.

Suddenly I hear voices behind me. Two girls in black spandex pants and nylon jackets are lifting a scull off the rack at the side of the rowing club. I turn from the railing and cut across the grass, up to the sidewalk. I walk along the narrow streets until my legs ache and my ears hurt from the cold. And then I go home.

Part Two

Winter

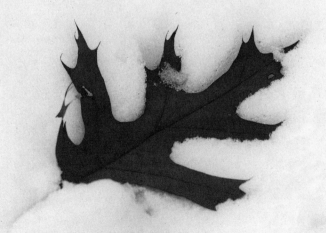

seventeen

10...9...8...

We're all around the television at Marissa's, watching as the last seconds of the year count down. Brendan leans against me, his chest against my back and his arms folded over mine, our fingers laced. It's too warm in here.

2...1.

"Happy New Year!" everyone shouts.

Brendan leans over and kisses me just below my ear. "Happy New Year, D'Arcy," he says with a smile, his dark eyes sparkling.

I shrug out of his arms and turn around. "Happy New Year," I say.

On TV someone is singing "Auld Lang Syne." All around me people are kissing and touching.

Brendan moves in to kiss me. Just before his mouth is on mine, I close my eyes and swallow. "We're gonna have a great year," he whispers.

I don't say anything at all.

*
**

I sit on the window ledge with my hands pulled up inside the sleeves of my sweater, trying to warm up my fingers. Behind me the window is hazy with frost.

Marissa pushes in beside me. "God, it's cold! Why do we have school anyway? Why don't they stick some kind of computer chip in our brain that has everything we need to know?"

I shrug.

"You ready for this?" she asks—we're having a history test—combing the long nails of her right hand through her hair.

I watch a few strands get loose and escape down the heat vent into whatever dark place there is below. Marissa is looking at me. Right. She's waiting for my answer. "I suppose," I say.

"Yeah, well how hard can it be? It's just a lot of boring dates and battles and dead people."

The bell rings. Marissa slides off the radiator and climbs over my desk to her own. I slip into my seat. Mr. Bailey already has the test papers coming down the rows. I take one and pass the rest back.

I read it all over quickly and then start the first essay without really taking any of it in. I haven't read most of the chapters. I haven't been to the library. I only have half a page of notes in my binder. But my hand is writing, making words, making sentences, filling the page.

*
**

I'm walking up Prince Street, my breath freezing in front of me. There still isn't any snow but the air is pinching cold. Maybe I should start wearing a heavier coat and a scarf or something.

I'm getting muscles in the back of my legs from all this walking. On the weekends I walk for hours, all over the city. At first I'd tell Mom I was going to Marissa's or to the library, but most of the time now, she doesn't even ask.

I follow the sidewalk where it turns right at the bottom of the old hospital. Up ahead of me some guy is running. He's wearing faded black sweatpants and an orange toque. His feet kind of swing out to the side as he runs, and the laces on his right-hand running shoe are loose. One of them whips against the pavement as he runs. Snap, snap, snap, but the rhythm is a little bit off. Sort of like his running. I imagine going up to him and counting out a beat—*one*, two, three, *one*, two three.

At the corner, the walk light is flashing its warning red hand. The guy runs in place, watching the traffic come down the hill and whip around the corner, watching—I'm guessing—for a chance to dart across between the cars. As I come up behind him, I realize it's Seth.

I touch his arm. "Seth?"

He turns and smiles when he sees it's me. "Hey, D'Arcy, hi."

"Hi. I...didn't know you were a runner."

"I'm not exactly. I'm training. I'm trying out for the track team."

The walk light comes on then and we cross, Seth jogging slowly beside me. "You're trying out for track?" I kind of make a face. I can't help it. "Why?"

"What? You don't think I can make the team?" His face is mottled from the cold. Or maybe it's the running.

"No, it's not that," I say. "It's just that you don't seem anything like the guys on the team—at least not the ones I know."

"What do you mean?" he asks.

"Well for one thing, whenever they see each other in the halls they make grunting noises and butt each other with their stomachs. They're like those mountain goats you always see on nature shows, except the goats bang their heads together."

Seth gives a big, fake sigh. "Okay, okay, no grunting in the halls."

"And they all have buzzed heads." I look over at the dark hair sticking out from under Seth's hat and curling over his collar. "Tell me you aren't going to cut off all your hair," I blurt. "I love your hair."

"You do?" He shoots me a sideways glance.

I feel my face getting hot and I know it's probably redder than my hat. "Umm, yeah," I mumble. "I do."

"All right. No buzz cuts either."

I step behind Seth to let a couple of women pass on their way down the hill. Seth pulls at the sleeves of his sweatshirt. "I better let you start running again," I say.

"Yeah, I've still got a couple more miles to do." He shrugs his shoulders a couple of times and swings his arms back and forth. "So I'll see you in math class."

I nod and he starts up the hill. His shoelace starts snapping on the sidewalk again. And then I remember. "Hey, Seth, I can do it," I call after him.

He slows and turns so he's running backwards now. "Do what?"

I mime the actions. "One hand to the other. Eyes closed." I've spent hours at night, practicing.

"I told you," he shouts, swerving at the last second to miss a garbage can someone hasn't dragged in yet. "You're ready for the next lesson. Meet me tomorrow before school, down by the bottom door."

"I don't think I can do two."

"You said that about one." He turns back around and starts to run faster as the hill levels off and takes another turn. "Tomorrow," he calls over his shoulder.

Tomorrow, I tell myself.

*
**

"I'll see you at lunch," I say to Brendan. The phone is jammed between my cheek and my shoulder. I'm flipping through my biology book. What the heck were we supposed to read anyway?

"Can't. I've got practice," he says. "So I'll pick you up."

"No. I told you I have to go early." There it is—the little piece of paper I stuck between two pages. Now I remember. We're supposed to read chapter 23.

"So, do whatever that math stuff is that you have to do at lunch."

"I can't."

"Why not? Jeez, D'Arcy, you're going to turn into one of those math geeks who can't even go to the can without a computer."

I don't say anything.

Finally Brendan sighs. "I'm sorry. It's just...I miss you."

What do I have to say so I can get off the phone? "I miss you too." I count pages. How long is chapter 23 anyway?

"So...I'll pick you up."

"I have to go early. Really. But we could do something Friday. After your game." Does he have a game Friday? I can't remember. I push the biology book off my lap onto the bed.

"Mmmm. What kind of 'something' did you have in mind?" Brendan asks.

"Umm, it depends on whether you win or not."

"Oh, we're gonna win. So be ready to celebrate." I hear noise in the background. "I gotta go," Brendan says. "Later."

I put the phone back in the base to charge the battery and turn off the ringer. Then I drop on the bed again, grab my bio book and scan through chapter 23, reading a paragraph here and there, just enough so I can fake it if I have to. I'm getting pretty good at that. I'm not getting all As anymore, but I'm passing everything. And nobody else seems to care, so why should I?

Enough. I shove the book in my backpack.

It's after eleven o'clock. It's funny how I don't seem to need to sleep anymore. Or at least not as much. I have so much energy. Too much to toss the beanbag from one hand to the other or lie around on my bed. I could call Marissa. She said

I could call her any time, but I bet she'd be pissed if I woke her up. Anyway, I don't want to talk to her.

I ease my way downstairs. I open every kitchen cupboard, looking for something quiet to eat. I settle on peanut butter and crackers. The peanut butter should make the crackers crunch less.

Why are there so many infomercials on TV late at night? Who's watching them? Okay, I am, but I'm not so stupid that I'd believe that brown goop is really going to look like hair when some bald guy spreads it on his head.

I find a show that's already started, dip crackers into the peanut butter jar and try to figure out what's going on. After a while I get it. The guy with perfect hair and too-white teeth killed his wife for her money. She had figured out what a scuzzbag he was and was going to divorce him to marry her real true love, who she should have married in the first place, but Shiny-teeth had come along and swept her off her feet. True-love knew she had made a new will leaving nothing to the no-good husband. And he knew it had to be hidden somewhere in her house, which had a gazillion rooms. He kept trying to sneak in and find it, plus prove Shiny-teeth was a murderer.

What I don't get is why she hid the new will in the house. She didn't have enough time to get a safety deposit box at the bank, but she had enough time to find a really good hiding place at home? Of course, if she'd been smarter, she wouldn't have married such a jerk in the first place and she wouldn't have ended up dead, which wouldn't make much of a TV show.

Just before the commercials, they flash back to the murder. The husband had made it look like a car accident, like she'd lost control of the car and gone over an embankment. Into the river.

I turn off the TV. It's a stupid show.

There's a wineglass on a square cork coaster on the coffee table by my feet. I don't know why, but I reach over and pick it up. The glass is about half full of white wine.

I don't drink. Brendan does—well, beer sometimes. I hate the smell of beer—it smells like a horse barn. And the taste is like hay and Ovaltine mixed together.

But the wine smells almost...woodsy. I make it swirl around the glass like they do on those snobby cooking shows. And then, without really thinking about it, I take a drink. It burns a little, and I cough as it goes down. But after a moment, warmth begins to spread out from my stomach.

There's another glass, with a little wine left in it, on the side table next to the lamp. Mark, my dad's friend, was here earlier, talking about money and stuff with my mom.

I finish that glass.

The wine bottle is on the kitchen counter with a couple of inches left inside. I drink it too. The warmth spreads through my chest and up into my head.

Warm. All I feel is warm.

And I don't feel anything else.

***

Seth is waiting for me by the bottom door of the school, just like he said.

"I don't think I can do this," I tell him. "I already told you I'm not coordinated, and besides, my hands are cold."

He slides down off the wall. "At least give it a shot before you give me your excuses." He's wearing a striped knit hat pulled all the way down to his eyebrows, and the collar of his jacket is up over his chin, so all I can really see are his eyes and nose.

I pull the beanbags out of my coat pocket. "Okay, show me again. What do I do?"

Seth takes both bags, and I jam my hands in my pockets again because I really am cold.

"Toss the first one up," he says. "Then just as it goes over the top, toss the second one." It really does look easy when he does it, but I remember from before when he showed me that it isn't. "Here. Now you try."

I throw the first bag up but…argh…it's too late. I end up with two bags in one hand. "I told you I can't do it," I say. Even though it's freezing, all of a sudden my hands are sweaty. I rub them on my jeans.

"You didn't drop anything," Seth says. His eyes kind of smile at me from under the edge of his hat.

I try it again. This time I manage to throw the second bag, but it flies off at a weird angle and lands on the sidewalk at Seth's feet. "At least you got both bags airborne this time," he says, bending down to pick it up. "Just keep practicing.

Everyone sucks at the beginning. You just need to find your rhythm."

"Wait a minute. I need rhythm to do this? Forget it then."

Seth smiles. "Everyone has rhythm, D'Arcy."

"Not me," I say. "Remember that hokey square-dancing stuff back in sixth grade?"

"Uh-huh."

I look down at my boots because it's still a bit embarrassing. "I flunked."

Seth leans over until he can see my face. "You can't flunk square dancing."

"Yeah, you can."

He shakes his head. "That doesn't count. Square dancing is really just follow the leader to cow music. You can *dance* dance, right?"

I shrug.

"Sure you can. Look, like this."

He starts to do some freakazoid dance right there on the sidewalk, kind of hopping from one foot to the other, punching his arms up in the air and bopping his head from side to side with his eyes closed.

"That's not dancing," I say, hunching my shoulders against the cold. "You're being a spaz on purpose."

He ignores me.

"And there's no music."

"It's in my head," he says without opening his eyes. "But for you I'll turn up the volume." He starts singing, "Oooh baby, oooh." He's trying to sing off-key, but the truth is his voice is good, deeper than I would have guessed.

I can't help laughing. "Stop." I grab his arm.

He opens his eyes and grins at me. Then he drops his arms. "I bet you can dance better than that."

"Yeah. I have Mr. Keating for homeroom and *he* can dance better than that."

Seth pulls off his hat and runs a hand through his hair. "So you can dance, which means you do have rhythm, which means you can learn to juggle."

I hold up my hands like I'm going to surrender. "You win," I say. "I'll practice."

He hands the other beanbag back to me. "Remember, up and over," he says.

I glance down the sidewalk. Three guys from the basketball team are coming toward us. I could make an excuse and go inside or just head up and hang around the upper door. But I don't. Because I don't want to.

Seth is telling me how he's going to have me juggling flaming torches one of these days. The guys pass us. Jaron, Matthew and Adam. They take up the whole sidewalk. Seth and I have to move to let them by.

"Hi, D'Arcy," Jaron says. He looks at me and then at Seth and then at me again.

"Hi," I say.

They're going to tell Brendan that they saw me with Seth. I don't care.

eighteen

Brendan's waiting at my locker, leaning against the wall with his arms crossed, when Marissa and I come down the stairs after our last class of the morning.

"Stud Puppy looks cranky," she says.

I turn my head and shoot her a look. She makes a face at me.

"Oh, go scratch his belly or blow in his ear and he'll be fine," she says.

We get to the lockers. Marissa has hers opened and her books stuffed inside in no time. "I'll find you later," she says. She eyes Brendan for a second and then she's gone.

"What are you doing here?" I ask as I put my things away. Like I don't know.

Brendan's big hand shuts my locker door. He snaps the lock. "I wanna talk to you," he says.

"Okay."

"Not here." He grabs my arm and pulls me down the hall and out the end door into the space under the breezeway where all the kids who smoke go to sneak one. He lets go and leans against the wall.

I tuck my fingers in my armpits. "It's freezing," I say. "What do we have to be out here for?"

Brendan doesn't answer, and he doesn't offer me his jacket. He grinds a couple of cigarette butts into the concrete with his boot. It doesn't matter how many times Mr. Connell prowls around out here; he can't catch the smokers.

Brendan finally looks at me. "Are you breaking up with me?" he asks.

"No." I shake my head.

His jaw moves like he's chewing on my answer. "So are you cheating on me then?"

"No." It's so cold I'm starting to shake. "What are you talking about?"

Brendan grinds another butt into bits of tobacco and paper. "Who's that guy you were with this morning?"

"Guy? You mean Seth? He's the peer tutor in my math class. I told you I had to come early for math." I shift from one foot to the other to try to keep warm. "Can we go inside now?" I start for the door, but he moves in front of it and grabs my arm.

"If you were doing math, why weren't you in a classroom?" he says. "The guys saw you just standing around."

I don't know why I want to pick a fight with him. I just do. "Have you got your friends spying on me now?" I ask, pulling my arm out of his grasp. "For your information, I missed a lot of stuff when my dad…I'm still behind. Seth's helping me because that's what the peer tutor does. If I'm going to get a scholarship, I need a good mark in math. We can't all get scholarships because we're good at some stupid game."

"I don't see why you can't get help in class from the teacher."

"Because it's what the peer tutor is supposed to do." Bouncing off all the concrete makes my voice sound louder than I mean it to. "What? You don't trust me?"

"It's not you I don't trust," Brendan says. I don't like his I-am-so-right tone.

"Seth wasn't hitting on me, Brendan," I say. "And even if he was, I can handle it. But he wasn't. Not every guy is a horn-dog like your friends."

Brendan reaches out and tries to take my hand, but I twist away. "Jaron and the guys were just watching my back," he says. "You standing around laughing with some jerk. It didn't look good."

"I don't care what it 'looked' like. I don't need your permission to talk to anybody. And I am done talking to you."

"D'Arcy." He takes another step toward me. Too close. I shove him, the heel of my hand on his chest. It catches him off guard and he almost goes over.

"Leave me alone," I say, my face close to his. Then I pull the door open and go inside. I listen for Brendan to come after me, but he doesn't. I keep on walking like I don't really care. Because I'm not sure if I do.

I hide out for a while in the third-floor girl's bathroom, sitting on the top of the tank with my feet pulled up.

I can't believe that fools teachers, but it does. After I figure enough time has passed that Brendan will have gone to the gym to shoot hoops with his buddies, I head down to my locker again.

When I get to the main level, I see Marissa and Andie in the stairwell below so I slip down the hall instead. As I come level with the auditorium doors, I hear music. Someone's in there playing the piano. Someone good.

He's playing jazz. My dad loved jazz.

I didn't get that music for a long time. I couldn't find the rhythm and I couldn't follow where it was going. Then one day Dad said, "Don't try to follow it or figure it out. Just let the music be all around you and listen."

And I did. I just sat there with my eyes closed and listened without thinking. The music ran up my back, it slid over my head, it jumped from one knee to the other and it spiraled down my arms. It was magic. I finally got why my dad liked it so much.

Now I turn the knob and push against the door with my shoulder. It isn't locked.

I shoot a quick glance around, but no one's looking at me. I open the door just enough to squeeze inside. Only three or four of the tiny stage lights are on, and it takes a minute for my eyes to adjust. Then I slip onto the side of the stage, staying close to the curtains so whoever's playing won't see me. The music is even better in here. It fills the room. At least that's how it seems to me.

The piano is almost at center stage. I take a chance and lean around the red velvet curtains for a peek...and suck in a breath that almost makes me cough, because it's Seth. He's sitting at that big black piano with his eyes closed, and his fingers are making that unbelievable music. I didn't know he could do that.

I just stand there. I don't try to hide but I don't move or say anything. I close my own eyes and feel the music. My throat is tight and tears prickle behind my eyelids, but at the same time I feel like throwing out my arms and twirling around and around and around.

When Seth finally stops, I open my eyes again and see that he's looking at me.

"How long have you been there?" he calls.

"I don't know." I blink and clear my throat. "A while." I cross the stage to the piano. "You're..." I don't have the right words to tell him how the music made me feel. "You're...wow."

He shrugs. "I haven't practiced for a while."

"You mean you can do better than that?"

He pulls one hand back through his hair. "It's not that hard."

I shake my head at him. "No, no, no. Don't tell me *this* is something I can learn to do if I practice."

Seth grins. "Okay, well maybe not in the first week." He swings a leg over the piano bench so he's straddling it. I sit on the end with my back to the piano. He's wearing the same sweatshirt he had on the day I saw him out running. God, why did he want to be on the track team with those zipper-head bozos when he could play like this?"

"You're really good," I say, leaning back against the keyboard. "So why don't you practice?"

Seth's smile fades and he looks out over the auditorium. "I've just got a lot of other stuff right now. I've been running a lot—you know, to get ready for the tryouts. They're next week."

"Why do you want to do that when you can play like this?"

"I...uh...I like it."

I remember the weird way his feet turned out when he ran and how his teeth had been clenched before he saw me that day on the sidewalk. I give him a sideways glance. "Really?" I say.

"Yeah. Running's good. You know, strong body, strong mind."

"Right. We all know what geniuses the jocks are."

"We're not supposed to even be in here," Seth says abruptly, pulling the cover down over the piano keys. "We should go before we get busted and..." He lets the end of the sentence trail away. Silence hangs between us like a curtain, and I don't know what to say to push it back.

I stand up and wipe my hands on the sides of my jeans. "Yeah. I'll see you later." I start across the stage without waiting for him. I don't know what I said that was wrong, but I know that something was.

✳
✳✳

"Whoa! What did he do?" Andie asks. "Run over your dog with his car? No. You don't have a dog. Boff the entire cheerleading squad? No, they're not *that* dumb."

"What are you talking about?" I say. Andie, Marissa and I are headed for our lockers.

"Stud Puppy." Marissa nudges me with her elbow and inclines her head toward our lockers. "What did he do? 'Cause whatever it was, he is in major suck-up mode."

I stop on the stairs and people push their way around me. Brendan is leaning on my locker, holding a bouquet of red roses.

Marissa elbows me again. "So what did he do?"

"We...uh...had a fight."

"You're getting flowers for a fight?" Andie asks.

"Hey. I've never even gotten a Hershey bar to make up for a fight," Marissa says. She shakes her head and continues down the steps, then stops and looks back at me. "C'mon, D'Arcy. Flowers? Don't just stand there and let them wilt."

Marissa and Andie get to Brendan before I do. The closer I get to the lockers, the slower my feet seem to go. "Nice flowers," Marissa says. "Whose lawn did you swipe them from?"

"Bite me," Brendan says, turning his head just long enough to give her the evil eye.

Marissa sticks out her tongue. Andie laughs. Brendan and I just stare at each other while Marissa takes out her purse and jacket. She turns and puts a hand to her forehead. "This is just"—she sniffs—"so touching." She squeezes her eyes shut and gives a couple of phony sobs. "Excuse me, but I'm overcome with emotions." She gives another fake sob and heads down the hall with Andie, hand on her heart.

"She's so weird," Brendan says. He never takes his eyes off my face.

"Yeah, I know," I say.

Brendan lets out a breath and then thrusts the flowers at me. "These are for you."

I shift my books to one arm and take the roses. There are six of them, with some of that little white flower that looks like bits from the end of a Q-tip. Everything's wrapped in crinkly green paper. "They're...beautiful," I say. They are, but since my dad's funeral I don't like flowers very much anymore.

Brendan takes a step toward me. "D'Arcy, I'm really sorry," he says. "Swear to God, I trust you." He pulls me into a hug, and I have to hold the flowers off to the side so they don't get squashed. He kisses the top of my head. "We're okay now, right?" he says against my hair. All I do is nod because I don't trust my mouth to say anything that will be even close to right.

nineteen

"Claire's here." Mom's waiting in the kitchen for me.

"What? Why didn't you tell me that she was coming?" I say as I pull off my coat. Claire is the last thing I need today.

"I didn't know. She called after you left."

"What does she want?"

"D'Arcy! She can come here any time she wants to. She is your sister."

"She never comes without a reason."

Mom sighs. She rubs little circles in the middle of her forehead with two fingers. I can see the pinched lines of a headache between her eyes. "She came to get the tea set. Your father wanted her to have it."

"Is she staying?"

"Just tonight."

Claire's in the dining room, sitting on the floor in front of the china cabinet, a stack of tissue-like paper on her right, a small cardboard box on her left, half filled with curlicues of paper. She's wearing khakis and a blue shirt with the sleeves pushed up.

"Hi, Claire," I say, leaning against the doorframe.

"Hi, D'Arcy." She half turns to acknowledge me. She's packing the tea set, setting each tissue-wrapped piece in the box.

"Need any help?" I ask.

"I can manage, thanks. I'm almost finished," she says, stuffing crumpled paper into the mouth of the teapot.

An image of my dad reading *Alice in Wonderland* comes into my mind. I'm nine, maybe ten, and he's reading the part about the Mad Hatter's tea party and doing all the voices. I feel a prickling behind my nose and eyes. I blink hard a couple of times.

"How's school?" Claire asks.

"Okay."

"Exams go all right?"

"Uh-huh. How's work?"

"Busy."

This is the limit of our conversations—the kind of nothing small talk you'd make with the person sitting next to you on the bus. Claire and I can't seem to connect. I stay there in the doorway, watching her, wanting, just once, to feel like family with her.

Claire gets up, smoothing imaginary wrinkles out of her pants. She slips past me and, automatically, one hand pushes the hair back from my face. "I'm going to need the other box," she says.

I turn and go up to my room.

I stay out of Claire's way as much as I can for the rest of the evening, which isn't that hard, because I think she's doing the same with me. I hear her take a shower about eleven o'clock and after that the house gets quiet. But I can't sleep. I slip downstairs thinking maybe I'll get something to eat.

There's a half-empty bottle of wine in the refrigerator.

I cut myself some cheese off a plastic-wrapped wedge and find an unopened box of sour cream–flavored crackers in the cupboard. Then I open the refrigerator again.

The cork comes out of the wine bottle with a soft pop, like pulling my finger out of my mouth. I take a drink right out of the bottle. And another. And another. And another.

The heat begins to spread out from my stomach. All of a sudden I don't care about Claire. I don't care about anything.

⁎

I'm at the table finishing breakfast when Claire comes down in the morning. She's carrying a tote bag and a caramel-colored coat over one arm. She reminds me of an actress in those old black-and-white movies they show at the Majestic.

The cartons are by the kitchen door. "I'm just going to put these in the car," she says. She leaves her coat and bag on the chair next to me.

I nod. My mouth is full of cereal so I can't say anything, which is good, because I don't have anything to say. A hand touches my shoulder and I jump, sucking milk into the back of my nose.

"I'm sorry," Mom says as I hack and sputter. "I didn't mean to scare you." She pats my back between the shoulder blades as I spray drops of milk across the kitchen table and try not to choke. "Claire's not gone yet?" she asks.

"She's putting the boxes in the car," I say when I can talk again.

Claire comes back in then. "Good morning, Leah," she says. "I thought I should get an early start."

"That's a good idea. But before you go, I have something for you." Mom offers Claire a small, leather-covered box.

Claire lifts the lid and stares at what's inside for a moment. Then her eyes go to Mom's face. "It's my father's watch."

"It was a gift from his father. I had it cleaned and adjusted. You're the oldest. I think you should have it."

My dad's watch. He always wore it. He put it on when he got up and took it off when he got into bed. He must have been wearing it when he died. How did she get it?

I can't get my breath. I press hard against my breastbone. Breathe. Breathe. Breathe.

"Thank you," Claire whispers. She clasps the box between her hands as though it were made of something breakable. She clears her throat. "I better get going," she says.

Mom drops one hand on my shoulder. "Claire, there's something I want to say to you, before you go."

She's going to tell Claire about Dad being sick.

"Leah, I really have to get on the road."

"I know you think your father didn't have any love left for you. That he abandoned you when he married me and we had D'Arcy, but it isn't true. He loved you just as much.

He wanted all of us to be a family. He hoped..." She stops for a moment, swallows. Her fingers dig into my shoulder. "He just ran out of time on that."

Claire shifts her weight from one foot to the other like she can't wait to get away. "Leah, I..."

I can't stop staring at the box with my dad's watch. I can feel my hands shaking in my lap. My mother continues talking as though Claire hadn't spoken. "You really hurt him. He was a good man and a good father. To both his children. He didn't deserve to be treated the way that you treated him. I hope you'll think about that. And I hope you'll remember that you still have a sister."

The silence spreads across the room like a pool of spilled water.

"Half-sister," I say. I'm actually surprised to hear the words come out of my mouth.

"D'Arcy," my mother says. I hear *Stop It* in her voice but I'm not going to.

"It's true," I say. "Claire doesn't want a real sister. Not me, anyway. She hates me."

"I don't hate you," Claire says, but she doesn't even look at me.

I get up and go stand in front of her. "It's okay. I don't like you either."

"D'Arcy! That's enough," Mom says, her voice loud and sharp.

"You don't deserve to have that." I point at the watch. "You didn't want Dad. Why should you have his things?"

Claire sighs and tucks her perfect blond hair behind her perfect tiny ear. "You're just a spoiled baby."

The remaining carton of china is right beside me. I bend down, flip up the flaps of the box and pull out the first tissue-covered piece my hand touches. I hold it high above my head and then smash it to the floor. I don't even know what I've broken, but I like the sound it made. "Goo-goo gah-gah," I say to Claire.

Mom is across the room in two steps. She grabs my arms and whips me around to face her. "What the hell's wrong with you?" she says. Her fingernails are pinching my skin. "You're going to replace that."

Claire is down on one knee, picking shards of china out of the crumpled paper. "You can't replace this. It's not something you buy at Wal-Mart." Her face is all sharp edges and pinched-together lines.

"Apologize," Mom orders.

I let my eyes slide off her face until I'm looking just beyond her ear. "No."

"Apologize to your sister. This is your last chance." She says each word precisely so I'll know she's not kidding.

"No," I repeat. "I'm not sorry and I won't say I am. You can ground me for the rest of my life. I won't say it."

"Then I will," Mom says. She forces me to face Claire, and I hear her teeth grind against each other. "Claire, I am sorry. Tell me what was broken and I'll track down a replacement."

Claire's face is white with anger except for a small red spot on the edge of each perfect cheekbone. It looks like someone has pressed their thumbs hard into the skin. "Didn't you hear what I said? This china is irreplaceable.

It was my grandmother's." She glares at me with angry, slitted eyes. "It was always supposed to be mine."

"I'll go online. I might be able to replace what's broken."

Claire stands up, holding the box of dishes. "I don't want a replacement, Leah." She looks around the room and shakes her head. "No wonder my father killed himself."

Mom's hand comes up and I think she's going to slap Claire, but instead her arm wraps around me, hugging me against her body. "Get out of my house, Claire," she says softly.

Claire doesn't say a word. She just walks out the door. In a moment I hear the car start and drive away.

There is a long silence. Mom goes to the counter and pours herself a cup of coffee.

"What the hell were you thinking, D'Arcy?" she asks, her back to me.

"She doesn't deserve to have Dad's watch. It's like you gave her a reward for being so horrible."

She turns, cup in hand. Her eyes are cold and there are deep lines around her mouth. "It's what he would have wanted me to do." She walks past me, out of the room.

twenty

Political science. I'm trying to listen. Trying at least to seem like I'm here. I make myself watch Mr. Lawrence's lips, try to concentrate on what he's saying.

"...family; Mom and Dad, two point three kids, a dog, a ranch-style bungalow and a station wagon. It's how a lot of people lived when your parents were kids, and it became the definition of a family. Does it work today?" He's sitting on the edge of the desk and he leans forward as he talks, pulling the class in.

Everyone tries to answer at once. "One at a time," Mr. Lawrence says, holding up a hand. "Kevin, go ahead."

Kevin sits sprawled in his seat, on his tailbone with his legs in the aisle. He can't get away with that in any other class. "No way."

"How so?"

"Families may start out like that, but they sure don't end up that way," Kevin says. "I mean, I have a mother, a father, a stepmom, a stepfather, two half-brothers and a stepsister."

"Good point. Andrea, what about you?"

"It's not fair."

"Why not?"

Andie gestures with her pen. "It says if you're not this one kind of family, then you're not a family at all. Where does that leave single-parent families? And what about people who aren't married? Or aren't related at all?"

"What do the rest of you think? Is that true?" Mr. Lawrence asks. "Do you have to be related to be considered a family?"

There are mostly "yeahs" and nodding heads around the room. "What about the Cane family?" someone shouts from the back. We've been studying twentieth-century crime. Joshua Cane had three wives and a bunch of kids. Nobody knows for sure how many people "the family" killed.

Laughter.

Mr. Lawrence holds up his hand. "Seriously, what about someone like Joshua Cane and his followers? Why do we call them a family?"

Words are coming from all over the room now.

I stare at the frost etched on the window. Then I realize that Mr. Lawrence is saying my name.

"D'Arcy, you're shaking your head."

I am?

"You don't agree?" he asks.

"It's bullshit," I say. "Don't you get it?" Everyone is staring at me. The bell rings. I gather my books and stand up. "It's all bullshit."

***

Mr. Keating hands me a slip of paper. "See Ms. Wilson at the guidance office."

"I have English class," I say.

"It's all right," he says. "Take that to Mrs. Young and then go." He looks...disappointed, as though he was expecting me to confide in him and I let him down because I didn't.

Mrs. Young glances at my get-out-of-jail-free pass and says, "Make sure you get the assignment from someone."

The guidance office is next to the main office. "I'm D'Arcy Patterson," I tell the secretary. "I'm supposed to see Ms. Wilson."

She points at the open door behind her. "You can go in."

Ms. Wilson is behind her desk, writing on a long yellow pad. About me? She's maybe twenty-five, with shiny dark hair pulled back in a bouncy ponytail. She's wearing a yellow sweater with embroidered daisies around the neck. Somehow I know that there's a daisy on the ponytail elastic too.

She looks up. "D'Arcy? Hi. C'mon in and close the door please."

Closed door. Trouble. I sit in the chair on my side of the desk.

"D'Arcy, the reason I wanted to talk to you is..." She pauses.

And I say, "Because I said 'bullshit' in Mr. Lawrence's class."

"Not exactly." Ms. Wilson smiles as though we're friends or something. "I'm sorry about your father. I just wanted to see if there's anything you need."

I shake my head. "I don't think so."

She looks down at her pad. "You caught up on the work you missed?"

I nod.

"And you're keeping up with your assignments?"

Nod again.

She looks at me. Here it comes. "Several of your teachers say you haven't seemed like yourself. You've been having a lot of stomach pains, the nurse tells me."

I grimace, swallow and put my hand on my stomach for effect. "Mrs. Sutton says it's stress—because of everything."

Ms. Wilson puts her elbows on the desk and leans forward. "I know it's difficult for you. Is there anything you'd like to talk about?"

With her? No. Nothing bad has ever happened in her perky ponytail life, I can tell. And I'm supposed to pretend she's my new best friend and tell her *how I feel.*

"Nothing you tell me will leave this room."

Oh yeah, right. She's giving me a look like a dog watching you hold a treat in the air, waiting for it to hit the floor. "It's just… hard, you know," I say. I look down at the floor for effect.

Ms. Wilson reaches across the desk and pats my arm. "I know," she says. "It takes time. Let yourself grieve."

Let yourself grieve? What teacher manual did she get that from?

I almost laugh. I turn it into a fake sob and add a little shudder. She keeps patting my arm. I count to twenty slowly in my head, then take a deep breath and let it out before I look at her. "Thank you," I say.

"I'm here for you, D'Arcy," she says. "Anytime you need to talk."

I'm here for you? I was wrong about Mr. Lawrence's class. That wasn't bullshit. But this is. I have to get out of here.

I do my apologetic face then, lips together, eyes down. "I'm really sorry I said 'bullshit' in class. I'll apologize to Mr. Lawrence."

Ms. Wilson gives me another understanding smile. "That's a good idea. But don't worry about it. I'm sure he's heard worse."

I stand up and give her my best almost-a-smile smile.

"Remember, you can come and talk to me anytime," she says.

I only make it down the hall and around the corner before I start laughing. Laughing and laughing until my knees go weak.

* * *

Marissa and I are sitting near the top of the double stairway that leads down to the front entrance of the school. Nobody ever uses those doors. They're so heavy it takes two people to pull them open, and that's after you've already climbed three sets of steps from the street. Then when you get inside, you have to climb more steps just to get to the center hallway.

I think the main doors are pretty much for show. Mostly everyone just hangs here on the steps until there are too many people, and then some teacher comes by and says, "Don't you kids have something better to do?"

"You wanna do something Saturday?" Marissa asks.

"I don't know," I say. "I've got a ton of math. And I've got that project for political science."

Marissa is eyeing some blond guy down by the doors—the baggy T-shirt, torn jeans, pierced, musician type she always goes for. "Oh, yeah, you're on Mr. Lawrence's shit list because you said bullshit in class." She elbows me. "Get it? Bullshit. Shit list." She smirks like she just came up with something brilliant. "So what did they do to you, anyway?"

"Just sent me to the guidance counselor, that's all."

Blond Guy has noticed Marissa, so now she has to look somewhere else as though she's not interested in him. "Which one? Mrs. Henessey or Malibu Barbie Counselor?"

"Ms. Wilson. Why do you call her Malibu Barbie?"

Marissa keeps darting little glances at Blond Guy. "C'mon. She has a tan in February. The only things faker than that are her boobs."

I pick at a hangnail on my finger. My nails look kind of raggy and chewed. I forget when I last did them.

Marissa jabs me with an elbow. "Who's that?" She tilts her head toward a guy who's stopped to talk to Blond Guy.

I look. It's Seth. I haven't seen him since the piano. He's missed the last two math classes. "That's Seth," I say.

"Isn't he some kind of student teacher in your math class?" Marissa asks, tugging the neck of her orange sweater.

"Peer tutor." I look away, but then I look back.

"He's cute," Marissa says.

"He's not your type."

Marissa leans back on her elbows, making her chest look

bigger, which is why she does it. "I've decided I want a guy who'll challenge my mind."

I turn to stare at her. "Do you want me to puke on your shoes?"

"I'm serious."

I just keep staring.

"I am." She makes a face. "Well, sort of."

I know Seth is looking at me before I turn my head. He doesn't smile or wave and neither do I. Marissa is still talking but I don't know what she's saying.

And then Brendan leans over me and slaps his hands over my eyes.

I start and suck in a breath.

"Guess who," he says in a goofy fake voice.

My neck stiffens. "I know it's you, Brendan," I say.

He drops his hands and sits on the step above me. "You're supposed to guess," he says. Then he leans down and kisses me on the mouth, even though we're not supposed to do that in the hallways. His tongue pushes at mine.

I pull away and look over my shoulder, but Seth is gone.

twenty-one

Somebody's smoking somewhere. I can smell it faintly.

I hate cigarettes. I hate the smell in my hair and my clothes, and I hate kissing someone who smokes—not that I've done it much. Brendan doesn't smoke, because he's an athlete and he has to look after his body. So no cigarettes. Beer apparently is different. All the guys on the team drink a lot of beer.

"Want some?" Brendan asks, sticking the can in my face.

I don't like beer. And I've only told Brendan that about two hundred times. But every time we're at a party, he still shoves the can in front of my face and says, "Want some?"

I shake my head. "No."

It's too warm in here. I shouldn't have worn this sweater, but Brendan was waiting—and talking to my mother, which isn't a good idea—so I just grabbed it out of the drawer and hauled it over my head. Plus Brendan is sitting right behind me on the arm of the sofa, his chest against my back, one arm around my waist, and he always gives off so much heat it'd probably be cooler sitting with my back next to the woodstove in the corner.

"I thought we were going to celebrate," Brendan says close to my ear.

I turn my face toward him. "I thought that's what this party's for," I say.

He kisses me on the mouth and smiles. "I mean just you and me," he whispers. He licks the curve of my ear. He thinks it's sexy. It isn't.

Brendan chugs the last of his beer. Then he lifts me to my feet and stands up himself. "Let's go," he says. "There's no one at my place."

"Where are your mom and dad?"

Brendan grins and gives me a little leer. "Some party thing at the hotel. I don't know what for. But they got a room—they're staying the night. So the house is empty." He hangs his arm around my shoulders and we start moving toward the door.

Crap. How am I going to get out of this? Is there any way I could puke? I try concentrating on it as we cross the deck of the cottage. Nothing. And I can't shove my finger down my throat. Gross.

I can't say I'm on my period. I've used that one twice. I wish I could just tell Brendan that I'm tired and I want to go home, but he'd take it the wrong way.

I'm still holding a bottle of orange pop. It's what I always drink at these parties. Except this time my orange pop is a little bit of orange and a lot of a wine cooler called Tropical Fiesta. I found it out on the deck and emptied it into my pop bottle. It tastes better than regular wine. I take a quick drink and then a second one.

Brendan drives with one hand on my leg all the way back into town, talking about basketball and a bunch of other stuff I don't really hear. I say "uh-huh" every once in a while between drinks, and that seems to be enough. And then we're at the house, we're in Brendan's bedroom—cleaned up, which means he's been planning this. I pop three orange-flavored Tic Tacs so he won't taste the wine. His mouth's on mine and his hands are up under my sweater. I can feel him breathing faster.

"I love you. I love you so much," he whispers.

I kiss him hard and use my tongue so he'll stop talking, and I hope he won't notice that I didn't say anything back.

A sound wakes me. I sit up in bed listening. Waiting. There it is again. Soft. Low. The hairs rise on the back of my neck. What is it? A cat? A raccoon? What else could it be? I'll get up. I'll look and it'll be nothing, just two cats on the lawn trying to date each other.

The living room light is still on. I step into the room and Mom is there, doubled over on the sofa. Her whole body is shaking, trembling uncontrollably as if she's having some kind of seizure.

I sway dizzily for a second, then get my balance and run to her, crouching at her feet. I put my arms around her. "What? Mom, what is it? What's the matter? What's wrong? Tell me what's wrong."

She makes a gagging sound and clutches her stomach. She is going to be sick. She is going to heave and there's no bathroom down here.

"Don't throw up here," I tell her. "Mom, don't puke!"

I pull her upright, start toward the stairs. She's still shaking. She makes another retching noise. *Not here,* I beg as I half drag her up the steps. There are too many. She's so heavy. Her feet slip on the treads and fall over themselves.

I can't let her fall. Another step. Another. Another. Another.

The top.

I pull her into the bathroom and lean her against the toilet, wedged between the bowl and the bathtub. I squat on the floor beside her, holding her shoulders. She retches over and over. The sound curdles my own stomach. Nothing comes up. It's just the dry heaves.

"Won't...come...up," she chokes out between gags.

What do I do? Should I make her throw up? Was this in first aid? I don't remember. I don't remember.

And then she vomits. I hold her head over the toilet and breathe through my mouth, looking away.

Oh God! Oh God, don't let me be sick, God, please don't let me be sick, I say over and over in my head.

Mom vomits again. I try to shut out the sound, the smell. I just hold on to her as hard as I can.

Finally there is nothing but empty retching. I reach up and flush the toilet.

I shift around so that I can hold her with just one arm across the front of her body, pull a towel down into the tub and douse it with cold water. I squeeze out as much as I can with one hand and fold it over into a lumpy roll. I hold the towel to Mom's forehead and then against the back of her neck. Water drips from one end down along my arm and seeps into the neck of Mom's sweatshirt. Slowly the retching eases and the trembling begins to lessen. I wipe her face and throw the towel into the tub. Her body suddenly slumps against mine, knocking me onto my knees.

She's crying. No sound, only tears, soaking her face. I hold her with both arms as tightly as I can.

I don't know what to do next. I don't know what to do now. I can't think five minutes ahead. I can't think five seconds ahead.

We can't stay here like this. Her body is a dead weight against me. "We've got to get into the bedroom," I say. I try to get her upright, but even though she is thin, she is still too heavy for me. I struggle into a crouch and move around so that most of her weight is against my left shoulder. "Help me," I whisper as I lift her, pushing with my legs.

Somehow I manage to get us both up and down the hall into the bedroom. I sit Mom on the bed. Her face is blotchy, her eyes are red and swollen, brimming with tears that spill over, slide down her face and drip off her chin. Her arms are pressed tight to her stomach. There are bits of vomit on her sweatshirt.

"Sit here for a minute," I tell her. "I'm going to call an ambulance."

"No." It comes out more of a moan than a word. She reaches for me with one hand. "No."

"You're sick. You need to go to a hospital."

"No." She rocks back and forth, eyes closed.

What do I do? What do I do? I want to run. I want someone else to do this. But there's only me. "All right," I say. "All right."

I pull off her clothes and dress her in a warm nightgown. I can see the outline of her ribs and her almost nonexistent breasts.

I get Mom into bed, turn on the electric blanket and roll her on her left side, wedging her in place with a couple of pillows so that she can't roll on her back, maybe vomit again and choke. That much I do remember from first aid.

I sit on the floor by her head. Eventually I hear her breathing change, and I know that she's asleep. I've been taking every breath with her. Now I lean against the side of the bed and stretch my legs across the carpet. Closing my eyes, I let my breathing find its own pattern. I stay there for a while longer, listening, watching, but she stays asleep.

There's a nearly full bottle of some kind of disinfectant cleaner in the cupboard under the bathroom sink. I pour half of it into the toilet bowl. Then I throw Mom's clothes into the tub with the wet towel and add water and the rest of the bottle.

Suddenly I can barely stand up. My legs feel like plastic bags of water. My mouth is dry, my upper lip sticks to my teeth. I look at my hands. They're moving as though they are being controlled by someone else. I sag against the sink, close my eyes.

No. C'mon, c'mon, I tell myself. *Get up. Move.*

I can't but somehow I do.

Downstairs I check everything twice—doors, windows, the stove. I can take care of us.

I get my robe and take the chair from my desk into my mom's room. She's still sleeping. Her forehead is cool. Her breathing is steady. I drag the big chair by the window close to the bed and settle myself in it, wrapped in a blanket, with my feet on the desk chair. It's not a bad bed. I know there are much worse ways to sleep in the world.

I've brought the broom upstairs with me. It leans against my knee. I wrap my hand around the wooden handle. It makes me feel better to hold something solid.

I sit there listening to the night sounds and the house's own rhythms and noises. I try not to think about anything at all, so I won't be afraid. Tomorrow this will all be over. I close my eyes for just a minute.

I wake up with a start. For a moment I don't know where I am, even as I have the sense that I'm not in my own bed. My head has flopped back and off to the side. Slowly I roll it down and around to the other side. Some of the knots release and the stiffness loosens.

I look over at the bed. Mom's moving in her sleep. She shifts and twitches, making small, hurt sounds. The blankets have slipped down off her shoulders. I get up, unwinding myself from my own blanket, and cover her, tucking the sheet against her neck.

Her sleep is still agitated. I kneel next to the bed and gently stroke her temple. Suddenly a memory is there in my mind: My mother is doing the same thing for me. I'm very little, sick with the measles or chicken pox. I'm hot and itchy. Mom's singing something about a dancing bear. The words aren't part of the memory, but the tune is there. I hum it, very softly. Mom's face relaxes, and she settles back into a quiet sleep.

It's cold the next time I wake up. Light's peeking in around the curtains, so it's morning. The quilt's slipped onto the floor. My skin puckers into goose bumps. I glance over at the bed.

Mom is gone.

I scramble out of the chair and run down the hall to the bathroom. The door is open.

No one.

I take the stairs two, three at a time, half falling. I have two hearts, pounding, pounding, one in each ear. And in my head I'm begging, *Pleasegodpleasegodpleasegod.*

She's in the kitchen, slumped against the counter.

"Mom, are you all right?" I ask, grabbing both sides of the doorframe for support.

"Yes." Her voice is raspy. Her robe is belted crookedly over her nightgown, one side hanging longer than the other. Hair sticks out in wisps all around her face, which is waxy pale. I can see the fine blue veins under her skin like rivers seen from the sky. In one hand she holds a cup of something. Tea? Water?

My legs go wobbly with relief, and I keep one hand on the wall for balance. "Go back to bed. I'll get you anything you want," I say.

"I am going. This is fine. It's all I want right now." She straightens up, pulling at her disheveled housecoat. "I'm okay." She clears her throat. Coughs. Swallows. "Thank you.

For taking care of me last night." She stares at me for a long moment. "You get that from your father," she says softly. "It's what he would have done. You're so much like him."

I blink away the tears that have come out of nowhere. "You...uh...you should see a doctor or somebody," I say.

She shakes her head. "I'm not going to bother a doctor. It was probably just something I ate."

"How could it be? We ate the same things and I'm okay."

"I had a sandwich last night. The tuna salad." She shrugs. "I guess it didn't agree with me."

"What tuna salad?" I cross the kitchen, open the refrigerator and root inside.

"Just what was in there. D'Arcy, leave it. It doesn't matter." She waves one hand at me.

I find a container and pull the lid off. The smell is rank and sour, worse than cat food that's been left in the sun.

I jerk my head back. Gag. "God! How could you eat this? It smells awful. Oh lord, and there's blue fur on the top." I throw the dish into the sink.

"I wasn't thinking." She pulls at her bathrobe again. "I was tired. I didn't pay attention. It was just a little food poisoning. You took good care of me, and I'm all right."

"I just don't know how..." I stop and swallow down the roiling in my stomach. "How could you have eaten that?"

"I was distracted. It's not a big deal. It's over now."

"People die from food poisoning." The words get out even though I don't really mean them to.

"Don't"—the word comes out sharp and angry. She closes her eyes for a second—"fuss. It's over. I'm all right." She doesn't look at me. "I'm going back to bed for a while."

I grab the end of the counter so hard my fingernails hurt. I have to keep holding on. I just have to keep holding on.

twenty-two

Seth isn't in math again. And I can't get past the first equation on the sheet Mr. Kelly handed out. I keep looking over at the door, hoping Seth will walk in late, and then I lose my place in the calculation and have to start again.

Mr. Kelly stops at my desk and smiles at me. Marissa says he's a hunk. Actually, what she said was, "You know, I could almost stand to take dork math with a hunk like that for a teacher."

Mr. Kelly is tall with blue eyes and dark hair and dimples when he smiles. It isn't until he starts talking about derivatives and integrals and the Newton-Raphson Method that you can tell he's a math nerd. "Having problems, D'Arcy?" he asks.

"A little," I say. "Do you know where Seth is today?"

The smile disappears and his eyes shift away from me for a second. "Seth has some personal things to take care of. He'll probably be back tomorrow."

"Is he all right?"

Mr. Kelly nods. "He's okay." He turns to the sheet of problems on my desk. "Show me where you're stuck," he says. His way of saying, I guess, that if he knows anything else about Seth, he's not going to tell me.

I manage to get all but the last equation solved by the time the bell rings. I head back to my locker the long way so I can walk past Seth's. He isn't there, and I don't see him in the halls or on the stairs anywhere.

"Hey, D'Arcy," Jaron says as he pushes past me, taking the stairs two at a time. I give him a wave as the back of his varsity jacket disappears around the corner. And then I remember: Today's the day they posted the results of the track team tryouts.

I think about Seth running up the hill, and the way his foot splayed out with every other step. Maybe that's why he missed class. Maybe he was pissed or depressed or something because he hadn't made the team.

After any kind of team tryouts, they always post the results on the bulletin board just outside the gym doors where everyone can see them. That way the people who made the team get to make the people who didn't feel like losers.

I head down the breezeway to the gym. There's a red sheet of paper tacked to the bulletin board. I scan down the list of names and, one up from the bottom, there it is: Seth Thomas. He made the team.

"D'Arcy?"

I turn around. Brendan, already wearing his red practice jersey and baggy gray shorts, wraps me in a hug.

I remember too late to hold my breath. Brendan only washes his lucky jersey when the season's over.

"Hey, you came to watch practice."

"Hi, umm…" Crap. Now what?

Brendan tilts my chin up and kisses me. "Mmm, I'm glad you're here, but you can't stay. It's a closed practice."

"Oh. How come?"

Brendan rolls his eyes. "Coach is going to ream us out for something."

I run my hand along his arm and make myself smile at him. "Then you better not be late."

"Yeah. Yeah, I gotta go." He pulls me against him again with his free hand and kisses me again. Then he lets go and takes off down the hall. "I'll call you later," he says over his shoulder.

I cruise past Seth's locker again. He isn't there. He isn't anywhere on that floor. Mr. Kelly is at the board, working on a string of equations with a couple of guys from our class, but neither one is Seth.

I walk back to my locker, put my books away and get my stuff. I go out the bottom door and head up the sidewalk, half expecting to find Seth sitting on the wall juggling. He isn't.

He isn't at the track either. I watch the runners for a minute. They all have such long legs and smooth, elegant strides in their black spandex runner's pants. There's no one with Seth's old gray sweatshirt and spazzy way of running.

It had seemed like such a big deal to Seth to make the team, so why wasn't he out there with the rest of them, running and freezing and sweating at the same time, pounding around the loop? I still didn't get why he would want to be a jock when he could play the piano that way.

The piano.

I go back into the school through the doors closest to the breezeway and head for the auditorium. There's no music this time, but still I want to check inside.

The door's locked. I twist the knob and push my shoulder against the wood, hoping it will somehow just pop open. It doesn't. He probably isn't even in there but...

I eye the doorknob. Brendan and Jaron used Brendan's bank card once to get the door to Jaron's parents' cottage open. They ended up breaking the card in half, but they got in.

I rummage in my backpack and find my library card. No teachers in the hall. I slip the card between the doorframe and the edge of the door. Nothing happens. It won't slide up or down. I can't move it from side to side and it won't go in any farther. This isn't going to work. I yank at the card, and for a second I think maybe it'll break too, but then I get it out.

Great. How come this door wasn't like the balcony doors to the auditorium, which didn't close all the way half the time? For a second I don't move. The balcony doors. What's the matter with me? I head upstairs again.

The left-hand side of the double doors opens as soon as I turn the knob and lean against it. I stand by the top row of seats and let my eyes adjust to the darkness.

The piano is still at center stage. But there's no Seth. I'm about to go when I see something move at the edge of the stage, a bit left of center. I ease my way down to the balcony railing, holding on to the end chair of each row. Someone is sitting on the top step to the stage, throwing something from hand to hand, up and over in a perfect arc.

I feel my way along the railing to the wall and find the stairs down to the main floor of the auditorium. I'm not even certain it is Seth until I'm almost to the stage.

He's cut his hair, not buzzed like the guys on the track team, but a lot shorter than it was. And he's wearing a suit. Well, part of one. The jacket and tie are on the back of a chair in the first row.

I stop at the end of the aisle because...because I'm not even sure I should be there. "Hi," I say.

Seth looks up. "You spending all your time in here now?" he says.

"I was looking for you."

He shrugs. "Well, you found me. Guess I didn't hide very well."

"Is that what you're doing?" I ask. "Hiding?"

"I'm just sitting, that's all. I like it in here. It's quiet." Back and forth. Back and forth. His hands never stop moving, never stop tossing whatever that thing in his hand is back and forth. I think maybe I could get hypnotized if I keep watching it.

There's something at the back of my throat that I can't seem to get down no matter how many times I swallow. "You weren't in math class," I say.

"No, I wasn't," Seth says.

He doesn't look right. He doesn't sound right. I feel a finger of fear crawl up my back. "You made the track team," I say. I try to make my voice happy as though maybe somehow Seth will catch the feeling.

He snatches the whatever-it-is he's been throwing right out of the air. "Whoopee," he says in a flat, bored voice. "Wow." He looks over at me for a second and then looks away.

"Yeah, whoopee," I say, anger sharpening my words. "Because you worked hard to make the team. You were out running all the time when it was, like, one hundred below. And you did it. And now you don't care?" I let out a breath. "I don't get it. What's wrong with you?"

Seth laughs. It isn't funny. The sound echoes around the auditorium, harsh and mean. "What's wrong with me? Me!" He slaps his chest with one hand. "Don't you get it, D'Arcy? I'm me. That's all I can ever be. That's what's wrong."

My legs are wobbling. I feel behind me and grab on to the arm of a chair. "I don't understand," I say.

He just stares. Not at me, at something out in the dark somewhere—something only he sees. The silence winds around us. "Go away," he says finally.

The metal edge of the armrest is cutting into my hand, but if I let go I think I might fall. "Maybe if you tell me what's—"

"Go away."

"I just…I just want to help." It's hard to breathe. The air has changed all of a sudden.

Seth shifts his eyes to me. "Get the fuck out of my face," he spits.

I take a step back, as though the words pushed me. Tears fill my eyes. I feel my way back a row and then another row. Then I turn away, arms tight against my chest, and I go.

*
**

What am I doing here? I think I'm stuck in some kind of hiccup in time. Brendan is squeezed in next to me on the sofa again. Any second he's going to offer me a drink of his beer. Again. The place reeks of smoke and it's too hot. Again. Jaron's wearing that stupid cowboy hat he always wears when they win a game. What does a cowboy hat have to do with basketball?

Don't Jaron's parents ever notice that their cottage smells like an ashtray? Don't they ever come out here?

I hate these parties.

I start to stand up. Brendan grabs my arm. "Hey, where are you going?"

"I'm just going to the washroom," I say, pushing his hand away.

"Hurry back," he says.

The only bathroom at Jaron's parents' cottage is off the kitchen. And somebody's already in it. I lean on the wall by the door, waiting. There are beer bottles all over the place and pizza boxes and empty chip bags. Whoever's in the bathroom has left their drink on the table. I pick up the paper cup and sniff what's inside. Lemonade?

I try a sip. It's not lemonade. It's some other kind of cooler. I take another couple of quick sips and put the cup back on the table before someone comes in and catches me with it. I've ragged on Brendan about his drinking a bunch of times. How would I explain this?

The table's dirty. This place is a hole. How can Jaron's

parents not know what's going on? What do the guys do? Come out here every Saturday and clean?

I get an image of Jaron and Brendan and the rest of those guys in aprons and hairnets, washing the counters and scrubbing the floors. Right.

"Hi, D'Arcy." Becca Jensen squeezes her way around the wooden table in the middle of the kitchen. She lifts the lids of a couple of the pizza boxes, I'm guessing she's looking for something to eat that hasn't been here since last Friday night.

"Hi," I say, but she isn't paying any attention. She's checking out the room, and I can't tell if she's looking for food or for someone to hook up with.

Whoever's in the bathroom is taking forever.

Ric and Dylan come in from the deck. They're laughing about something. "Okay, okay," Ric says. "My turn." He stops, swallows and lets out a long loud burp.

"Christ! How do you do that?" Dylan asks, shaking his head and fanning in front of his face. "That was foul."

Ric pats his stomach and smirks. "Talent, my man. Talent." He notices me then. "Hey, D'Arcy. Where's Brendan?"

"Living room." I point.

Ric drops on the corner of the table and pulls one of the open pizza boxes over. He grabs a slice, pinches it in half and crams most of it in his mouth. "Your brother gonna run track?" he says to Dylan, talking and chewing at the same time.

I lean over and bang on the bathroom door.

"Just a minute," a voice calls.

"Yeah," Dylan says, "it's pretty much the same team as last year. Except, do you remember that Thomas guy who used to run for St. Vincent's?"

A rushing sound fills my ears, like water is running somewhere close by.

"Yeah," Ric says. There's a string of cheese dangling off his bottom lip. "That's the guy who offed himself, right? About this time last year?" He snaps the pizza crust in half and shoves it in his mouth.

"Right. Well, his brother made our team. Pity vote. Matt says he can't even run. He's some kind of math geek."

I pound on the door again and this time it opens. "Jeez, D'Arcy, what're you in such a rush about?" Lindsey Waters asks. Her hair is pulled back in a sleek braid and her makeup looks perfect. Was that what she was doing in there?

I mumble, "Excuse me," move past her and push the door shut with my shoulder. The rushing sound fills my head. I stand in the middle of the tiny bathroom with one hand on the wall and the other on the rim of the sink and wonder if I'm going to pass out.

Seth's brother killed himself? Was that why—I lower myself to the edge of the old bathtub. Did Seth know about my dad?

Suddenly the room is too hot and too small. I open the door and work my way back to Brendan. He's talking to Ric, his hands flying all over the place.

"Brendan, I need to go," I say.

"We just got here," he says, not even turning to look at me.

"I feel sick."

He looks at me then, and I guess I look bad because he stands up and puts a hand on my shoulder. "You didn't eat that pizza did you?"

I shake my head and almost fall over. Brendan grabs me. "Okay, we're gone," he says.

I let him walk me to the car and do my seatbelt. Mostly I try not to think, because right now I don't know what to think. Brendan offers to come in with me when we get home, but he doesn't push it when I say no. Sick people scare him.

My mother isn't home. I don't know where she is, but I'm just as glad she isn't here. I throw my smoky clothes in the laundry hamper and get in the shower to wash the smell out of my hair. I keep all my thoughts about Seth pushed down as the water beats on my head. After, I pull on a sweatshirt and pajama pants and curl up in the rocking chair. Finally I let myself think about what Ric and Dylan said.

Seth had a brother who killed himself? Did he know about my father? How could he know? Did everyone know? Was he just being friends because he figured we were some kind of freak brigade? Why didn't he tell me? Is it all just a coincidence? It can't be. But why didn't he tell me?

Why?

twenty-three

"What's this about, anyway?" someone behind me asks as we file into the auditorium. "Who cares," says Kevin Mitchell from one row up. "Gets me out of English class."

I squeeze Seth's beanbags, jammed in my sweater pocket, and look over the railing trying to spot him.

"Why are we having an assembly?" I ask Marissa.

She looks around, then slouches in her seat. "Watch for Keating," she says, pulling out a sparkly pink lipstick. She checks out her reflection in the tiny mirror on the end of the cap, then remembers I asked a question. "Oh, it's some suicide guy."

I freeze. Marissa is still talking, but I can't hear her. All I can hear is the sound of my own heart thudding in my ears.

Sit up, I tell myself. *Breathe. Act normal.*

Mr. Connell makes a bunch of announcements—at least I think he does. I see his lips move, and everyone else seems to hear him.

The "suicide guy" is all in black—black jeans, black turtle-neck sweater. His dark hair is short and spiky as if he's always running his hands through it. He moves around the stage like some kind of TV evangelist revving up the crowd. And then I hear one word. Just one: Signs.

I can see my dad's face even without closing my eyes. Oh God, did I miss signs? Was he trying to tell me? He gave me his Red Sox cap the week before. I didn't know that meant anything. I didn't know. When he got back from Mexico, he slept almost the whole next day. I didn't know. I didn't know.

I'm shoving my way down the aisle, past people's knees, before I realize I've stood up. I make it to the girl's bathroom just in time to puke up my cornflakes. I rinse my mouth for a long time under the tap at the sink, but the sour taste won't go away.

When I come out of the bathroom, there's Seth, in jeans and his gray sweatshirt, leaning against the banister where the stairs start down to the second floor. He looks over at me, and I don't know if he's waiting for me because he saw me leave or if he bolted for the same reason I did. Neither one of us says anything. We just stand there staring at each other.

Finally he inclines his head toward the stairs. "Want to get out of here?" he says.

I nod.

He almost smiles. "Let's go," he says.

We walk without talking, up the hill behind the school, across the square. Seth seems to know where he's going. Me, I don't care.

I don't even know this part of the city well, but Seth obvi-ously does. When we get to the old stone wall at the back of where the hospital used to be, he stops and boosts himself up onto the ledge. It's like a higher, longer version of the wall around the old part of our school. He leans down and offers me his hand. I put my other hand on the top of the wall and pull myself up. Behind him I can see what looks like a path through the scraggly trees and bushes. Seth starts along it, still holding my hand.

We come out in an open area. The grass is long, dried yellow and brown, beaten down by the winter, stained with dirty snow in the shaded places. I can see part of what I'm guessing is the old foundation from the hospital poking out of the ground. Some crumbling bricks along one side make a kind of alcove. It's surprisingly warm in the sun. He lets go of my hand then, and I rub my palm with my fingers, missing the warmth of his already. Seth sits down and brushes off a place for me.

The city is spread out below us like something built of blocks and toy cars. Up here it seems so small, and I seem so big.

I study Seth's face. His eyes are red and there is dark stubble on his cheeks. "Why didn't you tell me about your brother?" I ask.

He clears his throat but keeps staring straight ahead. "I thought...you might have known. There were a lot of rumors last year...when it happened."

"How..." I stop, press my lips together and start again. "How did you know about my dad?"

"I just...I just figured it out...from the way they wrote about what happened in the paper...it was the same way they wrote about my brother. They didn't say he killed himself but…" He lets the sentence end, unfinished.

"And what? You figured we could be friends because we're both some kind of freak?" My voice is getting harsher and louder. "Because your brother and my father…you thought we should start hanging out?"

"No!" Seth swings to face me and sucks in a shaky breath. "I thought you would understand. I thought that I could talk to you and you wouldn't ask any questions or give me that pity look I get from everyone else. I thought maybe we could be friends and it would be normal."

Tears prickle in my eyes. "You should have told me," I say in a soft voice.

Seth studies my face. "And then what?" he asks. "Would you have wanted to be my friend?"

I can barely choke out the words. "I don't know."

He turns away from me and looks out over the city again. I can't stop shivering. I pull the sleeves of my sweater out through the arms of my jacket and down over my hands. Then I press my hands between my knees to keep warm.

There's garbage scattered all over the ground around the old stone foundation, bits of paper wrappers, coffee cups, beer cans, empty wine bottles. One of the bottles near my feet is broken, almost into two even pieces, as though someone had just snapped it in half.

Seth lets out his breath in a soft sigh. "That afternoon we'd had a fight," he says. "About who ate the last piece of pizza. I was so mad." He looks down at the ground. "Can you believe it? Mad over a stupid piece of pizza. I took off out of the house and I said, 'I'll be glad when you're gone. When you leave for university, I'll be so happy I'll have a big freakin' party.' That's the last thing I ever said to him."

"But you didn't really mean it," I say.

"No. But I couldn't take it back."

I put my hand out, hesitate, and then touch his arm.

"I wish I'd said, 'Man, I'm glad you're my brother.' I wish I'd asked what was going on in his life, if he was okay. Mostly, I wish he wasn't dead. Every day I wish he wasn't the one who was dead."

I take a shaky breath. "The night before...I was at the door and...he hugged me and he kissed the top of my head and...and...he said, 'I love you so much,' and...I...I...I was in a hurry and so I didn't say it back. I just said, 'Me too, Dad,' and...and would it have killed me to say...to say the words?" I look away. "He had...he had a disease... ALS. It's...it's bad and I keep wondering, did he think we wouldn't love him anymore if we knew he was sick?" The tears slide down my face and drip off my chin.

"I tried to be perfect after Eric died," Seth says. "I tried to be like him. He could do anything. He was one of those people that just...shined. Just being around him, you could feel it. He didn't even mean to kill himself. He was at a friend's house and they were just goofing around with this gun. I wanted to make up for it—you know, for my mom and dad. But I couldn't. You can't make up for that kind of thing."

He reaches for my hand. "Last week was the one-year anniversary of Eric...dying."

"The day in the auditorium."

Seth nods. "Yeah. I'd just come from the memorial service. I told my dad I'd made the track team, and you know what he said? Nothing. He just looked at me and turned and walked away."

"He was upset. He didn't mean to—"

"Yes, he did. And I don't blame him. My father ran cross-country in high school. He was good. Nationally ranked good. Summer after graduation, he broke his leg. He could still run but he was too slow. Eric was as good as Dad used to be—maybe better. It was my dad's second chance." He shakes his head. "You think I don't know that the only reason I made the track team was the pity vote? I'm not a jock. I'm not Eric. Every time my father looks at me he sees what he lost."

"Is that why you cut your hair?" I ask.

"Yeah. Dad was always after me to keep my hair short like Eric's. He always said my hair was 'artsy-fartsy.' He didn't even notice I got it cut."

"Was there stuff we didn't notice?" I asked. "Back there at the assembly, that guy, he said there were signs. Did I miss them? Was there some way I could have stopped him?"

Seth just stares at the ground. After a moment he gives a slight shrug. "I don't know," he says.

Silence.

"Sometimes I wonder where my dad is now," I say softly. "What he is. What he's feeling. If he even has them anymore. Is he in heaven or hell? Or are there even such places? Maybe he doesn't feel anything. Maybe he's nowhere. Maybe he's just nothing." I take a breath and let it out. I can't sit anymore.

I wipe my face with the sleeve of my sweater and stand up. "Let's go," I say.

"Where?"

I look around. "I don't care. I just want to walk." My bottom lip is shaking. I can't talk about this anymore. "Can we do that? Please?"

Seth looks up at me. He nods slowly. "Okay." He gets to his feet, and for a second we just stand there. Then Seth reaches for my hand. And I give it to him.

We walk around for hours without talking very much. Seth buys fries from a chip wagon and we share them, holding the cardboard plate between us. Slowly we work our way back down the hill. We stop at a bench by the water a couple of blocks from school.

"You know we're going to be in trouble for just taking off," Seth says.

"I don't care," I say.

"Connell will probably call your house. What's your mother going to say?"

I kick a piece of broken pavement over the lip of the sidewalk. "I don't care about that either."

He rubs his thumb over the back of my hand. "There's some stuff I have to do, but I'll walk you home first."

"No, it's okay. It's not that far."

We both stand up. Seth is still holding my hand, and I don't want him to let go. "So, I'll see you," I say.

"Tomorrow," Seth says.

I give a quick nod.

He smiles then. For the first time all day, he smiles. "Okay."

He squeezes my hand. "Tomorrow," he says again.

He jams both hands in his pockets, gives me one last long look and heads down the sidewalk. I watch him for a minute, and then I head off in the opposite direction.

My stuff is still at school. I don't want to go in, though. I don't want to see Mr. Keating or the Malibu Barbie guidance counselor or anyone like that. So I lean against one of the big maple trees by the corner across from the school and watch for Marissa.

She comes out of the door with Andie. Crap! But Andie just stands there long enough to flip her hair out from under the collar of her jacket. Then she heads for the student lot.

I watch for a break in the traffic and then cut across the street from corner to corner. I don't want to get any closer to the school. If Marissa's going home, this will be the way she comes.

She turns then and does start down the sidewalk toward me. I wait, hands in my pockets until she glances ahead and sees me.

"Where have you been?" she says. "You never came back. What'd you do? Fall into a black hole in the bathroom or something?"

"I was sick," I say.

Marissa frowns, studies my face. "Okay. So where'd you go? You didn't go to the nurse's office. Keating was pissed. He sent me to look for you."

"I don't want to talk to him right now," I say. One of my knees keeps jerking back and forth, back and forth. In my pocket, I press my fist hard against my leg. "Could you go back and get my stuff out of my locker for me?"

"Yeah, all right." She pulls the strap of her courier bag over her head and hands the bag to me. "Hang on to this," she says.

I point over my shoulder, across the intersection. "I'll wait over there for you."

Marissa stares at me for a second. "I'll be right back," she says and then heads toward the school.

I wait, back against one of the trees that line the sidewalk, and it seems like forever until Marissa returns. She hands me my backpack and the little woven black purse she gave me for my birthday last year. I give her back her own bag.

"Thanks," I say.

"Are you sure you're all right?" she says.

I tuck my purse inside my pack and sling it over one shoulder. "Yeah. I'm just hungry."

"Want to go to Gallaghers?"

"I think I'll just go home," I say.

Marissa opens her mouth, then presses her lips together again like she was about to say something but changed her mind.

"Thanks for getting my stuff."

"What's going on with you?" she blurts.

"Nothing. I told you I was sick." My leg is twitching again. I dig my knuckles into my thigh to make it stop. "I have to go."

Marissa steps in front of me. "You're lying, D'Arcy. I know you weren't sick. I know there's something going on with you that you won't tell me."

I look past her at the knobby peeling bark on the tree and bite the inside of my cheek so I won't get mad and say something I shouldn't. "There's nothing going on."

Marissa takes a step sideways so I have to look at her again. "That's a load of crap," she says. "I know you."

"You don't know anything," I say. Then I turn and walk away very fast. I hear Marissa calling my name, but I just keep walking.

I'm almost a block away before she catches up to me. She grabs my arm. Hard. Her nails pinch even through my jacket.

"Why are you acting like this?" She's almost shouting and half out of breath from running after me.

"I don't know what you're talking about," I say, wrenching my arm free. I jam my hand back in the pocket of my jeans so I won't rub the place where she grabbed me.

"Yeah, you do. You've been different since your dad died."

She tries to touch me again. I step back.

"Look, I'm really sorry about that. It sucks."

I press my lips together. Clench my teeth.

Marissa stands in front of me, feet apart, both hands gripping the strap of her bag where it cuts across the front of her body. When I don't talk, she shakes her head. "You're my best friend, you know. But you're turning into somebody I don't know. You're scaring me."

I take a couple more steps back. I don't want to listen. And I can't talk to her. She isn't going to understand. Not about my dad. Not about my life. "Just leave me alone," I say.

My voice sounds far away, like it's coming over one of those tin-can-and-string telephones I used to play with.

Marissa moves closer. "Talk to me," she pleads. "Please, D'Arcy."

I feel something heavy and dark pressing, pressing inside of me. I try to push it away, push Marissa's words away, but she's right in my face now. I turn my head away.

Just as fast she shoves my shoulders. "D'Arcy, stop it! Stop zoning me out. Talk to me! Talk to me!"

"He killed himself!" Through my teeth, over my lips. Somehow the words get out, angry, loud and hard.

Marissa is frozen in place, her eyes filled with tears, her arms hanging as if her anger has just blown away. I keep looking at her until she looks away, and then I go. This time she doesn't follow me.

twenty-four

I kick off my boots, drop my stuff on the table and open the fridge door. There isn't much in the refrigerator. I settle for bread and Cheez Whiz that's about as easy to spread as orange Play Doh. I lean sideways over the sink and eat so I don't have to use a plate, and I have a couple of mouthfuls of red wine and then drink some orange juice from the carton to get rid of the taste.

I'm on my second piece of bread when the doorbell rings. "Go away," I say, even though the person out there can't hear me.

It rings again, and then a third time. Standing in the middle of the kitchen, I can still hear it. I go to the front door and look through the peephole.

Marissa.

"Go away," I whisper.

She pushes the bell once more. I open the door, and we stare at each other through the screen.

Her eyes are red-rimmed, and the shiny pink lip gloss she always wears has been chewed off. "D'Arcy, I'm so sorry," she says. "I had no idea your dad…" She doesn't finish.

Did she ring my doorbell four times just to tell me something I already know?

"I know you're upset. I understand now."

"No, you don't." Did I say that out loud? "I'm sick of people saying they understand when there's no way they can."

She sucks in a shaky breath. "I want to help."

I smack the screen with both hands. She jumps.

"Stop," I shout. "Doesn't anyone hear me when I'm talking? You. Don't. Understand." I spit each word at her. She winces. "You don't know how I feel. You can't help me."

Her eyes fill with tears. A couple slide down her cheek. "Just let me come in," she pleads. "Just…just talk to me. Please, D'Arcy."

I put my hands over my ears and shake my head hard. "I don't want to talk." I want to scream at her, but if I do I might never stop. I suck in my top lip and bite it hard before I open my eyes. "You can't ever understand. So leave me alone."

I slam the door and lean against it. After a minute I look out the living room window. Marissa is leaning against one of the railing posts on the verandah. I can't see her face but her shoulders are shaking. I think maybe I hurt her feelings, but there isn't any way I can fix that.

*
**

It's after seven o'clock when my mother gets home. I hear her moving around downstairs but I just stay on my bed with my chemistry book. I'm not studying or anything, but it looks good.

She walks into my room without knocking. "I thought we agreed, no more cutting class," she says. No "Hello dear, how was your day?" I know by her voice that she's pissed. Not that she's yelling or anything like that. When she's mad, her voice gets flat and steady. That's how I know.

"I was sick," I say.

"I know what the assembly was about, D'Arcy," she says.

"I was sick," I repeat.

"I understand why you didn't want to sit through that. But you can't just disappear for the whole day. You're grounded—for the rest of the week and this weekend. I straightened things out at school. You pull something like this again and I won't." She picks at a piece of loose skin on the side of her thumb. "It happened, D'Arcy. Life goes on. We have to go on."

I just sit there, silent.

As my mother turns to go, she says, "I found a plate, to replace that one you broke, from one of those discontinued china places online. I've ordered it to be sent to Claire. You owe me seventy-six dollars altogether."

"Claire said she didn't want a replacement."

Mom stops. Her shoulders tense. "I don't care what Claire said. You will replace what you broke."

I push my chemistry text aside. "She didn't deserve—"

She doesn't let me finish. "Seventy-six dollars, D'Arcy. I want it by the end of the week."

***

"What are you doing?"

My mother's voice makes me jump. I'm by the back door, lacing up my black boots. I turn and look up at her in the doorway. She's changed into jeans and a gray sweatshirt.

"I'm going for a walk," I say, standing up.

"You're grounded." She bites the end of each word. "You're not going anywhere."

I put on my beanie hat and pull my gloves out of my pocket.

"D'Arcy, did you hear what I said?"

"Yeah," I say. I zip up my jacket. "I'm going for a walk."

Mom grabs my arm. "You're not leaving this house."

A rushing sound fills my head, like the beating wings of a thousand hummingbirds. "I'm not listening to you anymore." I hear my voice getting louder. "You never listen to me. I don't have to listen to you!"

She lets go of my arm as though it was suddenly hot. "D'Arcy, go to your room." She says each word slowly, as though I were deaf or stupid.

"No. Do you think anything you say matters to me anymore?" I'm shouting. "Yeah, I ran out of that assembly. Then I ran to the girl's bathroom and puked up my breakfast. You didn't want to hear that. You grounded me for getting sick." It's hard to get my breath.

"And…and how long did it take you to find that…that stupid plate for Claire."

She doesn't say a word. She just stands there, arms hanging by her side.

"You're supposed to be on my side, Mom. Not hers. She didn't deserve anything." Tears are making everything blurry. "You gave her Daddy's watch. You took it off of…. and you gave it to Claire. How could you do that?"

The pain hits as though someone had come up behind me and taken a good whack at my head with a two-by-four. I want my dad. "Oh God, oh God, oh God," I whisper over and over, pressing my hand to the back of my head, digging in the fingers.

"D'Arcy," Mom says. She tries to put her arms around me but I push her away hard. She stumbles against the side of the kitchen table. "Listen to me," she starts.

But I talk right over her. I am full up to the back of my throat, full of words and feelings that I've swallowed, and now there isn't enough space left inside to hold it all. I am vomiting words.

"I don't want to listen to you," I shout, right in her face. "I don't want you. I want Daddy. Why did I have to be left with you? I hate you."

Mom's hand snaps out like a whip, cracking the side of my face. In all my life, no one has ever hit me.

The coffeepot is sitting on the counter next to the sink with a puddle of cold coffee from this morning still in the bottom. I grab it and fling it against the wall. The glass smashes into dozens of tiny pieces, just the way my life has.

I run out of the room and just keep on going. Out of the house. Away.

I walk across the park, up one street and down another as it gets darker. I end up at the Majestic without even thinking about it.

I check the pockets of my jacket and find a wadded-up twenty in the little inside zippered one. I join the end of the line that's edging toward the box office. I don't bother looking up to see what movie's playing. I don't care.

Someone touches my arm. "D'Arcy?"

I suck in a breath and take a step back, bumping the woman ahead of me. "Sorry," I mumble, holding up a hand to show her I wasn't trying to knock her down on purpose. I see the wheelchair out of the corner of my eye before I get completely turned around.

"It is you." Andrew smiles up at me from the chair. "I didn't mean to scare you. I just wanted to see if you're all right."

I can barely hear what Andrew's saying. In my head I see the man, that day at the meeting, with the drool going down his face, except it's not his face. It's my father's.

I take a step back. Andrew reaches out his hand—the one with the brace. For a second I don't see his hand, I don't see him in the chair. I see Dad. "D'Arcy," Andrew says. But I don't hear his voice. I hear my dad's.

I turn and run.

I run until my chest burns, until every breath scrapes like sandpaper. I run until my legs start to shake. I have to keep moving. I keep my hands in the pockets of my jacket, jammed against my stomach to help hold me together.

My dad is everywhere inside my head. I can see him. I can hear him.

The car. His foot on the gas. That long bank down to the water. I see him undoing his seatbelt. I see the car rolling over and over. My eyes are open, but I can see it. Was there time to know it was the last second of his life? And if there was, was he sorry? Did he think about me?

My legs finally give out. I bend over, hands on my shaking knees, and try to catch my breath without puking. When I straighten up, I see that I'm at the top of the hill, beside the wall of the old hospital, where Seth and I were this afternoon. I pull myself up and look for the gap in the bushes where the path starts. I follow it up the rise. Back to that partly broken section of wall.

I sit and tuck my legs against my chest, wrapping my arms around them to stay warm. No one'll care that I'm here.

After a few minutes, a girl walks over to me. "Got any cigarettes?" she asks.

I shake my head.

"Just one?"

"I don't smoke. Sorry."

"It's okay." She smiles at me. "They kill you, anyway."

I watch her go back to her friends—another girl and three boys clustered around a bench under a dim streetlight on the slope near the old hospital driveway.

She must be cold. She's wearing a baggy pair of painter's pants and a stretched-out old pink sweater with the sleeves pulled down around her hands. I watch her talking to the others; the way she stands, legs apart, the breasts she barely has shoved forward.

They're passing a bottle around. I watch it going around the circle and think about having a drink, that heat burning away the ache in my stomach, burning away all of these feelings I don't know what to do with. Maybe I should go talk to them.

One of the guys takes a long pull from the bottle, then says something, and the girl who was looking for a cigarette laughs really loud and tosses her head so all the uneven layers of hair around her face fly out. He gets up and takes a couple of steps in my direction. She grabs his arm, but he swings her around and suddenly he's doing the grabbing.

He kisses her on the mouth, hard, pulling her head back with one hand caught in her hair. The others laugh. She shoves him away, then spits and wipes her mouth against her shoulder, which brings more laughing. He sits down again, but I see him look over at me as he does.

My pulse starts to twitch in the little hollow space at the bottom of my neck. I lean forward and search the ground for the broken bottle I remember from this afternoon. When I find it, I pick through the few small shards of glass from the middle, where it broke. I find a piece about three inches long, shaped like an arrowhead with a jagged point. I fold my hand carefully around it, the point extending beyond the crease of my thumb. Then I curl up on the old foundation again.

After a while, I don't know how long, I hear an engine and the sound of a muffler that's not working right. I look up the slope to the road and see an old van pull up and stop at the turn. Kids are clustered around the back door before it even opens. I hear voices and more laughing. I turn away and watch the lights down below on the bridge. I count sets of headlights.

I'm up to eighty-three when I hear someone coming. I tighten my fingers around the piece of glass in my hand, reassured by its sharpness.

I move only my head, slowly sideways, to see who it is.

"D'Arcy?"

Seth. My body goes slack with relief, and I realize I'd been hoping to somehow find him here.

"What are you doing here?" he asks.

"I had a fight with my mother. I just started walking and this is where I ended up." I don't want to tell him what happened at the Majestic.

"Here." Seth offers me a steaming Styrofoam cup, then sits down next to me. "It'll warm you up." He has a blanket rolled up under one arm. "You want this too?"

I shake my head, tuck the piece of glass in my pocket where I can get it quickly, and take the cup in my empty hand. It's hot chocolate, with a heap of little marshmallows floating on top.

"What's that van?" I ask, gesturing up toward the road.

"That's the Chuck Wagon," Seth says. "For Father Charlie, who drives it. He goes all over the city with food, coats, blankets and other stuff, for kids who need it. Sometimes I ride shotgun." He shrugs. "You know, to help him out."

"That's nice." I sip the hot chocolate.

"Father Charlie's the one who introduced me to jazz.

Charlie Parker. Oscar Peterson. He has all these old vinyl records."

"I thought all priests listened to was hymns and Gregorian chants."

Seth smiles. "Father Charlie's not a real priest. I mean, he used to be, but he's not anymore."

We sit in silence for a while. Seth tilts his head back and looks up at the sky. "Look at all those stars," he says. "Some of them are already dead, you know. Burned out a million years ago. It's taken all that time for the light to get here."

I turn my head so I can see the sky too. It's filled with stars.

"Father Charlie says that when you remember someone who's dead, it's just like the light coming from those burned-out stars. There's something of them left, still shining."

"I like that," I say.

The wind comes up suddenly behind me, sending an empty burger box skittering past us. I jump at the sound, slopping the steaming hot chocolate onto my hand. I drop the cup, press my hand to my mouth as tears fill my eyes.

"Did you burn yourself? Are you all right?" Seth leans over me.

I shake my head.

"Let me see." Seth takes my hand, pats it dry with the hem of his jacket and gently examines the skin.

I wince and suck in a breath. He lifts my hand to his mouth and kisses the place that was burned.

I know what's going to happen, even as the moment stretches between us. Then Seth leans in and kisses me on the mouth.

His lips are soft and warm. I kiss him back and he tastes like oranges.

We keep kissing and one of his hands is in my hair and the other is pulling me against him. I know where this is going and I'm not going to stop. I don't think about whether I should or I shouldn't. I don't think at all.

twenty-five

My mother's waiting in the living room, curled in a corner of the sofa in her robe, with a mug of something—coffee maybe—propped on her knees. "Where were you?" she says.

"Out."

She stares at me without speaking for a long time, long enough that I have to fight the urge to squirm. "Okay," she says finally. "If that's how you want to do it. Fine."

Yeah, this is how I want to do it. I go upstairs without answering. I turn on the lamp in my room and pull my sweater over my head. That's when I notice my Mp3 player is missing. It was on the bed when I left and it isn't there now.

I go back down the stairs. Mom hasn't moved. "Where's my Mp3 player?" I ask.

"I took it," she says.

"You can't take my stuff," I say, clenching and flexing my

fingers behind my back because I don't know where to put the anger I suddenly feel.

"When you pay me the seventy-six dollars you owe me, you'll get it back." She lifts her mug and carefully folds her robe over her knees.

"I'm not buying a stupid plate for Claire."

"Then I'll sell your Mp3 player and get the money you owe me that way."

"You go into my room and steal my stuff just to pay for a plate that Claire is never going to use anyway. And that she shouldn't even have."

I want to throw something. Behind my back I link my fingers, squeezing my knuckles until they hurt so I won't grab the lamp and hurl it across the room. "How many times did Claire come here for Christmas? Or Thanksgiving? Or anything else? Claire should get nothing because that's what she gave."

My mother's nostrils flare as she takes a breath, but it's the only hint that she's angry. "It doesn't matter what Claire did or didn't do. You had no right to do what you did."

Rainbow swirls of color dance in front of my eyes. "Fine," I shout at her. "Take it. Take all my stuff. Like I care."

I storm upstairs into my room, stand in the middle of the floor, half out of breath, and look around. My CD player. My mother gave it to me for my birthday. I unplug the speakers, carry the pieces one at a time down the hall and set them outside Mom's bedroom door. Then I go back for the pillows on my window seat and then the blanket from the back of my rocker and my fleece hoodie and the glass witch's ball that hangs in my window. I leave everything my mother has given me in a heap in front of her bedroom door.

And then I go to bed.

*
**

I wonder if Seth will be waiting for me as I start down the hill to the school in the morning. He is, sitting on the wall by the bottom door of the school, juggling three polished wooden balls. I clap when he finishes, and he dips his head in my direction.

"Hi," I say, suddenly feeling awkward.

"Hi." He catches all three balls and stuffs them into a side pocket on his backpack.

I don't know what to say. Things are different with us now. But I don't know what it means. I realize I'm shifting my weight from one foot to the other, swaying from side to side.

Seth leans forward and tucks a stray curl of hair behind my ear. His finger lingers on my cheek for a moment. And it's as though time is holding us there, the same way it did last night when he kissed my hand. "I'm going to remember last night for the rest of my life," he says, locking eyes with me.

I nod. "Me too," I say softly. I'm not sure if this is an ending or a beginning. Then he smiles at me and there, finally, is the Seth I've been trying to find for days.

*
**

Mr. Keating gives me his mournful, I'm-disappointed-in-you horse face again. I have the urge to laugh as I go past his desk.

I bite the inside of my cheek so that I'll look sorry. Because I'm really not.

Marissa is avoiding me. She wasn't waiting at the lockers like every other morning. But I see her watching me all through the announcements when she thinks I'm not looking.

What would I say to her anyway? She can't understand me or my life anymore. I wonder if she's told anyone about my dad. I could just say she's lying.

I sleepwalk through my morning classes. I take notes I probably won't ever look at. In English we have a quiz on a book I'm not sure I've read. At lunchtime I leave the school and just walk around. I'm pretty sure I won't be eating lunch with Marissa and Andie anymore, and I don't want to sit in the cafeteria by myself like some loser. And anyway, I'm not really hungry.

Math is my last class of the day. Seth is already there, working at the front of the room with Mr. Kelly. I stop just inside the doorway and watch them while everyone else files in around me.

Seth takes a stub of chalk and starts writing rapidly on the board. Mr. Kelly watches, arms folded, head tipped a bit to one side. Seth underlines one equation, says something and taps on another with the chalk. Mr. Kelly nods and begins to smile. Seth keeps scribbling. Mr. Kelly's head is going up and down now like a bobble-headed doll. Seth scratches out one last equation and then sets the chalk on the ledge.

The bell rings. I find my seat. Mr. Kelly explains the problems and sends the worksheets around the room. I'm on the second problem when Seth leans over my desk.

"Hi," he says. "You doing all right?"

He looks so different with his hair short. He looks good, but I liked it long. "Yeah," I say. "I pretty much understand it all."

He looks at my work for the first problem, following my figuring with one finger. "Okay, that's good," he says. "Watch out for number five. It's kinda tricky."

I circle five on my worksheet. Seth watches me, his eyes on my face almost like he's trying to memorize what I look like.

"Can you wait for me after class?" he asks all of a sudden.

"Sure," I say.

"Good." He moves up the aisle before I get a chance to ask why.

When the bell rings, I take my time gathering up my books. Seth is across the room, one elbow on Tim Mullen's desk, explaining something. I drop my worksheet on the growing pile on Mr. Kelly's desk. He turns from the board and smiles at me.

Out in the hallway, I lean against the wall by the door and wait for Seth. People stream by me, headed for the stairs, talking, laughing. I see Jaron and Ric coming from the Language Lab with Becca. The guys are too busy talking—Ric's walking backward and gesturing with one hand—to notice me, but Becca waves and calls, "Hi, D'Arcy."

I raise one hand in a wave back. And then...oh crap. It hits me. Brendan. I haven't talked to him or even thought about him in the last day and a half. What am I going to do? What do I say to him?

How can I...I can't explain about yesterday. And how can I tell him that Seth and I...I can't tell Brendan anything about Seth and me. Is there a Seth and me? I don't know.

And I don't want to talk to him about my dad. He won't understand any better than Marissa did. Oh God. Would she tell him? Something does a belly flop in my stomach. Did he call last night?

"D'Arcy?"

I give a start and drop my math notebook.

"Hey, I'm sorry. I didn't mean to scare you," Seth says, bending down to pick it up.

"No. It's okay. I was just kind of spacing out," I say, taking the book from him.

"I...uh...have something for you," he says, swinging his backpack off his shoulder. He leans one knee against the wall next to me and props the bag on top so he can root around inside it. "Here."

He holds out a stack of CDs. There are six altogether, held together by an elastic band.

"What are these for?" I ask, taking them from his outstretched hand.

"They're for you."

"I know that. Why?"

"Because I want you to have them," he says.

I slide the elastic off and check out the CD covers. Diana Krall in Paris. Oscar Peterson's "Canadiana Suite." The last CD in the stack has no paper cover. "What's this one?" I ask.

Seth gives me a half smile and shrugs. "That one's me."

I have to swallow down the sudden lump in my throat. "I...uh..." I run my fingers over the jewel case. "Thank you. This is the best present I've had in a long time."

Seth smiles. "I have to go," he says. For a second I think he's going to say something else, but he doesn't. He swings his bag back over his shoulder and walks away down the hall.

twenty-six

I don't head for Brendan's house on purpose. I walk around after school, mostly because I don't want to go home and maybe run into my mother, and somehow I find myself on his street. I make myself go ring the doorbell. There's a squeezing, aching knot in my stomach. Maybe he isn't home. But he is.

"Hey, babe, c'mon in," Brendan says.

He's wearing jeans and his red school sweatshirt, and his hair is damp. I remember when seeing him used to make my heart race. Now it just makes my insides hurt. When did that change?

I shake my head. "Uh-uh, I can't stay."

He grabs the waist of my jeans and bumps my body against his. "Nobody's home."

"I like it out here."

He runs his finger down my neck and down between my breasts. "I bet you'll like it in here better."

I push his hand away. "Brendan. Cut it out."

He just looks at me, a long look without saying anything. People seem to be doing that a lot all of a sudden. Or maybe they were always doing it and I just never noticed. I notice different things now.

I turn away from him and go sit on the front steps of the porch. Brendan comes out and sits down, squeezing next to me on the step. I slide down one so there is more room. I think I'm getting a little claustrophobic. I need more space around me.

"I need to ask you something," Brendan says.

I look at him. He is staring straight ahead. "Okay." I wait.

"Do you still love me?" He finally turns his head and looks right at me.

Why did he have to ask me that? "Why are you asking me that?" I say. "Because I didn't want your hand up under my shirt?"

He sighs. "Just tell me. Do you?"

I'm quiet almost as long as he was before he asked the question. "I don't know," I say at last.

I watch his Adam's apple bob up and down as he swallows and breathes out. He's stopped looking at me again.

"I'm sorry." I put my hand on his leg. I can smell his skin, clean from the shower, and that spicy deodorant he uses. I know it's important to explain. I'm just not sure that I can.

"It's not you," I say, rubbing the toe of my shoe over a bare spot on the step below me where the paint's worn off. "I don't think I love anyone right now. There are a lot of things I'm trying to figure out."

"What things?" He sounds angry. I glance up at him. His jaw is clenched.

"Stuff about my dad."

"I know it's been hard since your dad...died. But I thought by now things would be getting back to normal."

"I don't know what normal is anymore." That's the truth. "I feel like this is all I'll ever be. I've been waiting to be normal again." I laugh and get to my feet. "Waiting for normal. I don't even know what that is."

"He was a jerk," Brendan spits.

There is a *whump, whump, whump* sound so loud in my ears I must have heard him wrong. "What did you say?" I ask.

Brendan's head whips around to face me. "I said he was a jerk. Your father was a jerk."

"That's an ignorant thing to say." I'm almost out of breath. "My father was a wonderful person."

"Yeah. So wonderful he killed himself. He was a coward. He didn't give a shit what that would do to you."

I feel like someone's sitting on my chest. "You...knew," I manage to choke out.

"Yeah. Your father was a loser. I knew."

My left hand hits the side of his face just below his eye. I get the side of his head with the other one. "Shut up," I say. "Shutupshutupshutup!" My arms are swinging wildly, and I can't manage to hit him again before he grabs them and pushes me away. I stumble down the last two steps.

"What's the matter with you?" Brendan shouts.

"You're the loser," I fire back at him.

He jumps down the steps. He's breathing hard. "D'Arcy, I'm sorry. Okay? I'm sorry."

He tries to hold my hand, but I pull it away. "You're wrong about my father. He...he was sick."

Brendan grabs my shoulders and swings me around. "Okay. Okay. Whatever you say."

"He was sick."

"It doesn't matter. I'm here. I love you." He is almost whispering now. He tries to put his arms around me, but I shove him away as hard as I can.

"I don't love you." It comes out louder than I meant it to.

Brendan closes his eyes for a second. "You don't mean that," he says.

I can feel the tears running down my face. "Yeah, I do," I say. Then I turn around and start walking.

I go home. What else is there to do?

Seth's CDs are in my backpack. I don't have any way to play them. Now I wish I hadn't put my CD player in with all the other things I dumped in the hall in front of Mom's bedroom door.

By six o'clock it's pretty obvious she isn't coming home for supper. I prowl around the kitchen, looking for something to eat. It's pretty obvious she hasn't bought groceries for a while either. There are a couple of rolls wrapped in waxed paper in the bread box. They're hard and dried out, but there's no blue fuzzy stuff growing on them. In the fridge I find one slice of plastic-wrapped cheese. The edges are like white plastic, but the middle part is okay. And hidden behind the cornflakes box in the cupboard, I find a can of cream corn.

I heat the corn in the microwave and nuke the roll too until it's soft. Overall, not a bad supper. I've hit three of the four major food groups.

I eat in front of the TV, flipping between the Channel 7 news team, the Shopping Channel and reruns of *The Simpsons*.

The house is so damn empty. So am I. It doesn't matter what I eat. Nothing fills the hole inside me. I miss my dad. I miss the way he always sang just a tiny bit off-key. I miss his stupid jokes. I miss the way his beard always scraped my cheek, even if he'd just shaved.

There's wine in the refrigerator. I walk from room to room, drinking from the bottle, but this time it doesn't work, it doesn't burn away the aching empty feeling inside me, no matter how much I swallow.

In my room I lie across my bed in the dark, holding on to Seth's CDs with one hand. When my dad was here, nobody ever ate stale bread and cream corn for supper. It was never this quiet. It was never this dark and cold and empty.

twenty-seven

Math class. No Seth. Where is he? I keep shooting glances at the door. Midway through the class, someone knocks. We all turn at the sound. Malibu Barbie counselor is in the hallway. Mr. Kelly steps outside to talk to her, and we eye each other while we pretend to work, wondering who did what.

Mr. Kelly comes back in and looks around the room. His face has no color. It's as if all the blood has gone somewhere else in his body. He looks at me. Standing there in the doorway, he keeps swallowing and swallowing. He just stands there, like his legs don't work anymore, and he looks at me.

I hear myself taking shaky breaths. *Look somewhere else*, I say in my head. But he doesn't.

Finally he finds his voice. "D'Arcy—" He stops and clears his throat. "D'Arcy, may I see you for a moment? Outside."

I get up.

"Bring your things."

Everyone's eyes are on me. My heart's racing, trying to jump out of my chest. My hands don't work. I knock my math text on the floor, and when I bend over to pick it up, I bump the desk and my pencil rolls off into the aisle. I scrabble around on the floor and manage to gather up everything.

It feels like a mile from my desk to the door. I look out into the hall and I keep my eyes there. I don't look at Mr. Kelly. "Keep working on those problems," he tells the class. Then he closes the door.

I hold my books tight against my chest, like a shield between us. He takes a deep breath and lets it out. "D'Arcy," he begins. "It's…you need to go wait in the guidance office."

"Why?" I ask.

Mr. Kelly's face is ashen. It really is a color, I realize, not just an expression. "Your…uh…your mother's on the way. She'll explain."

"Why can't you explain?"

"Just go down to the office."

"No." I've never talked back to a teacher in my life. "It's about Seth, isn't it?" I say. I don't know how I know that, but I do. Maybe it's because Mr. Kelly is so upset.

He looks down at the floor for a second. "I'm sorry. I know…you two…were close."

"Was Seth in an accident? Was he out running? Did a car hit him?"

Mr. Kelly rakes a hand back through his hair. "Your mother will be here—"

"What happened to Seth?" When he doesn't answer, I ask again, only louder. "What happened to Seth?"

Darlene Ryan

"Seth tried to kill himself last night," Mr. Kelly says quietly. "He's in the hospital...it isn't good."

I hear the words but they don't make any sense. It's as though he's said them out of order. "No," I say.

"I'm so sorry."

I take a step back from him. "Seth...No."

"Your mother's on her way and—"

"No. You have this all wrong." My voice echoes down the hall. "He wouldn't. Did she tell you?" I gesture over my shoulder. "Malibu Barbie? No."

Mr. Kelly reaches out a hand toward me. I back way up and hold up my own hand to ward him off. Wordlessly I shake my head. It sounds like I'm crying or something, but I'm not because they've got it all wrong.

"D'Arcy, please." Mr. Kelly's eyes are red, as if he's going to cry.

"No!" I throw my books at him, and then I turn and run.

My fingers can't make the combination on my lock work. I remember when that happened and Seth came and opened it for me.

It isn't true.

I finally get the lock open. I grab my jacket and purse and head for the outside door. There must have been some kind of accident. That's what it was. Ms. Wilson is just too stupid to get it right.

It isn't true.

Maybe they'll fire her over this.

I cut across the street. I'll just go to the hospital and I'll find Seth and I'll tell him what she's saying about him.

It isn't true. Then I'll come back here and I'll tell Mr. Kelly and I'll make Ms. Wilson take back what she said.

It isn't true.

A tear slides down to the corner of my mouth. I swipe at it with my hand. This isn't sad.

It isn't true.

I stop at the information desk just inside the hospital doors. "Seth Thomas's room, please," I say.

The woman behind the counter is wearing some kind of blue smock thing with a red volunteer button pinned to the front. Her hair is in perfect tight gray curls all over her head, and her glasses are on the end of her nose. She looks like somebody's grandmother, and she probably is.

She types something—probably Seth's name—and watches her computer screen. "I'm sorry, dear," she says after a moment. "I don't see anyone by that name."

"He would have just come in, not very long ago."

"Oh," she says. There's a clipboard by her elbow. She runs her finger down the page and stops about halfway. She looks up at me. "He can't have any visitors, dear. Sorry." She looks past me and smiles at a man in a suit who is carrying a bouquet of flowers wrapped in green tissue.

I wait until she's typing on her computer again. Then I head for the elevators. The up arrow pings on just as I get there, and one of the sets of elevator doors opens. I step inside and push the button for the fourth floor. I've been able to read upside down since I was ten.

Seth is on four, southwest. There's a different color for each direction away from the elevators. I follow the green line.

It takes me to the nurses' station. How am I going to find Seth's room?

There's some kind of receptionist sitting behind the curved counter. I wait until she's on the phone. Then I walk over. "I'm looking for Seth Thomas's room," I say, keeping my voice low. "I'm his sister."

She has the phone wedged between her ear and her shoulder. She flips through a stack of papers in front of her. "Four seventeen," she says. She points down the corridor to my left. "Your family's in the waiting room down at the very end."

"Thank you," I whisper. I walk down the hall watching the numbers next to each door. 405. 407. 409. 411. There's no 413. I come to a small waiting area. A blond woman is sitting alone on an ugly orange vinyl chair. She's leaning her head back against the wall and her eyes are closed. I'm about to walk past when I notice she has Seth's gray sweatshirt on her lap and his backpack underneath her chair.

I walk over to her and touch her shoulder. "Excuse me," I say. She opens her eyes, blinks a few times and straightens up. "I'm sorry to bother you...um...are you Seth's mother?"

"I'm his aunt," the woman says.

"I..." How do I explain this? "They said at school that he...that he was here. Is he okay?"

"Excuse me. Who are you?" the woman asks.

I jam my hands in my pockets because all of a sudden I don't know where to put them. "I'm D'Arcy Patterson. I'm... Seth and I are friends."

"You're D'Arcy." She looks away. She's twisting her right index finger with her other hand as though she's trying to twist the skin off.

"I just was wondering if I could see him for a minute," I say.

She presses her lips together and slowly turns back to me. "He's on a respirator," she says slowly. "Only his mom and dad are..." She lets the end of the sentence trail off.

The room begins to go dark from the edges in. The woman grabs me and eases me into a chair, pushing my head forward. "That's it. Nice and easy. Just breathe." She keeps one hand on my back.

I concentrate on breathing. In and out. In and out. The darkness slowly disappears, and after a couple of minutes I sit up.

"You all right?" she asks.

I nod. "Could I just see him for a minute?" I ask. My voice sounds strange—raspy and thick.

"I'm sorry. The only people allowed in are his parents."

"I don't understand. At school they said he..." I can't say the words. But I can see from her face I don't have to. She knows what I mean.

"You know about Seth's brother."

"Yes."

"It's been very difficult for Seth—for his whole family. Just days ago it was the one-year anniversary." She clears her throat. "He...um...He wanted you to know he was sorry."

Everything is blurry. "How...how..."

"There was...a note."

"I don't understand." I reach out blindly with one hand and she takes it. "I thought he was okay. Yesterday he even gave me—"

An image of that guy, the suicide counselor from the assembly, flashes into my head. "You need to be aware of the warning signs," he'd said. "Depression. Sleeping a lot or not at all. *Giving things away.*"

Oh God. No. The CDs. I press the heel of my hand hard against my mouth because I'm already screaming inside. I get up, shoving Seth's aunt away with my other arm. The tears roll down my face into my mouth and drip off my chin onto my jacket.

She reaches for me. "Please, D'Arcy, come sit down," she pleads. Her voice sounds as though it's coming from the bottom of a very deep well.

I have to see Seth. This has to be some kind of mistake. I run out of the waiting room and down the hall. If I can just find his room. 420. 422. 424. The numbers swim in front of me. Where is it? My nose is running. I wipe it with the sleeve of my jacket and keep checking numbers. Somehow I'm lost. These rooms don't have any beds. There are no nurses.

I turn another corner. *Quiet Room* the sign over the door says. I don't know why I open the door and go in. I don't want anyone to find me before I can find Seth.

It makes me think of a church even though there's no stained glass and no crosses. There's one light at the far end shining down on a wall hanging of a sun all orange and yellow and red. Under the sun there's a long wooden table and rows of chairs arranged in semicircles.

I walk down to the first row of seats. If this is a kind of church, then maybe…maybe God will hear me. Maybe this is one of the places where he listens in.

I sit down, bow my head and fold my hands. The only prayer I can think of is "Now I Lay Me Down To Sleep," and that doesn't seem right. "Please, God," I finally whisper. "If you're listening, please help Seth."

I can't think of anything else. My head hurts and my eyes feel as though there's dirt in them. I lay my head down on the next chair, pull my legs up and curl into a little ball.

twenty-eight

For a minute I don't know where I am. My legs are cramped.
I stretch them slowly and sit up. How long was I asleep?
I don't have my watch. My eyes are puffy and raw. I rub at
them but it doesn't help.

Out in the hall there's a big window, and I can see it's
getting dark outside. I still need to find out where Seth is.
Seth's aunt has everything wrong.

I start walking, watching for the room numbers next to
the doors. I don't want to ask for directions because I don't
want to answer anyone's questions. Eventually I turn a corner
and go through a set of swinging doors, and I'm back at the
elevators.

Seth's aunt is there. All of a sudden my feet won't move.
She's leaning against the wall, hugging Seth's shirt and crying.
A gray-haired man has his arm around her shoulder and his
face close to hers. Not just any man. A minister.

When my father...a minister came.

No.

Seth can't be...No.

There's no air in here. I back away and bang into the stairwell door. They both turn at the sound.

"D'Arcy!" Seth's aunt takes a step toward me.

I can't talk to her. I bolt down the stairs, down until there's no more down. I come out the bottom door into the hospital parking lot and run. I run until my legs cramp and I have to lean against the side of a building for a few minutes until I can move again.

I walk up one street and down another as it gets darker. I don't know where to go or what to do, so I just keep walking. I end up on the hill without planning it. Or maybe some part of me did. I pull myself up onto the wall and find the path through the bushes. Farther up the hill some kids have a bonfire. The burning wood snaps, and sparks jump into the air above the flames.

My legs and hands are shaking. I sit on the ground and watch them tremble. I know it's cold, but I don't feel cold. All I feel is a dull ache in my chest.

I hear voices, shouts, laughing, the van coming and going. I just sit. And then, I don't know how long I've been there, I hear footsteps coming through the grass. I don't move. I don't care.

"I know you," a voice says. It's the girl from the other night, the one who was looking for a cigarette. This time she's wearing baggy overalls and a grey hoodie. "You don't smoke," she says.

I shake my head. She turns to go.

"You got anything to drink?" I ask.

She turns back to me. "Maybe."

"I have money," I tell her. "A little, anyway." I fumble in my purse and pull out a twenty. There's more than that but I might need it later.

She eyes the money. "That's not going to get you much of a party—four or five cigarettes and maybe a bottle if you're lucky."

"You can keep the cigarettes," I say.

Her eyes flick up to my face. "Shares on the bottle."

I nod. "Yeah."

She grabs the twenty from my hand. "C'mon," she says.

I follow her up the hill to the road at the top. The broken pavement curves down around the hill. At the first turn there's another fire burning in a metal trash can. Farther back off the road, I see a wooden picnic table. Two guys are sitting on top of it. A third is lying on the bench, arms folded behind his head.

"Stay here," the girl says to me.

She heads across the grass. I fold my arms across my chest and watch her. She talks to one of the guys sitting on the table. They're arguing. She holds up one hand and shakes her head so hard her hair whips across her face. He shrugs. She says something else but he ignores her. Finally she holds out the money. He snaps it from her fingers, and it seems to somehow magically disappear.

The other guy slides off the picnic table and starts toward me. The girl follows. He walks past me like I'm not even there and heads toward an old, dark-colored truck parked off the road under the trees. A yellow port-a-potty is tied in the middle of the truck. He climbs into the back of the truck and unlocks the potty door.

"Cool, huh?" the girl says. "What cop is ever gonna search a toilet?"

The guy's holding a plastic bag now. "Hey, Harmony," he calls. "Here."

She gets the bag and comes back to me. "C'mon, let's go," she says.

We walk back along the road and down the hill again. Harmony picks her way around the broken foundation until she comes to a place where there's a corner section of wall that stretches over our heads. "This is a good spot," she says. "Nobody much comes down here because it's kinda cold, but this way we won't have to share with anyone else." She hands me the bag and starts shoving garbage out of the way with her foot.

There are five cigarettes in the bag. I hand them to Harmony. "You sure?" she asks.

I nod. "Yeah."

She tucks four of the cigarettes into the front pocket of her hoodie and pulls out a book of matches. She lights the other cigarette, takes a long drag from it and closes her eyes. Smoke streams out of the corner of her mouth. She opens her eyes and catches me watching her.

"Yeah, I know they're bad," she says with a shrug. "But I figure, to hell with it. You gotta die from something. Right?"

The wine bottle has a screw top. I wipe my hand on the front of my jeans and twist it off. The first mouthful makes me choke and cough. Harmony whacks me between the shoulder blades a couple of times. "You okay?" she says.

I nod and wave her away. I take another drink and then another. It burns all the way from the back of my throat to my stomach. I offer Harmony the bottle. She wipes the top on her wrist and takes a couple of swallows, then hands it back.

I take another drink.

Harmony uses her foot to scrape a clear spot on the cracked concrete. She sits, hugs her knees to her chest and takes a drag from her cigarette. I hand her the bottle again and make a place for me to sit down against the other wall.

For a while we pass the bottle back and forth without talking.

Harmony puts her cigarette out on the concrete and kicks the butt away. She leans back against the red brick wall, tucking her hands in the kangaroo pocket of her sweatshirt. "So what's your name, anyway?" she asks.

I don't want to be me anymore. I look down the hill at the cars circling the harbor along Water Street. A nursery rhyme suddenly pops into my head:

Jack and Jill
Went up the hill
To fetch a pail of water.
Jack fell down
And broke his crown
And Jill came tumbling after.

I look at Harmony. "Jill. My name is Jill," I say.

Harmony lifts the wine bottle like she's toasting me. "Hey, Jill," she says. She takes a drink, then hands the bottle back again. "I'm Harmony."

I set the wine bottle on the concrete, tent my hands on top and lean my chin on them. The bottle wobbles for a second but stays upright. "Harmony. Like the song?" I ask.

She shakes her head and her hair flies into her face again. "No. Like everybody loving each other and not fighting and stuff."

"I thought it was the song," I say. "Old song—my dad used to sing—'Harmony and Ivory.'" Now I've said it out loud, it doesn't sound right. "No, that's not right. It wasn't Harmony, it was Emony." I start to laugh because it feels like there're bees buzzing in my head, and I can't get the word out the way I want it. "Not Emony," I say. "Enemy...no...Enum—"

I have another fit of giggles and my chin slides off the wine bottle. The bottle hits the concrete and starts to roll. Harmony and I both grab for it. She gets it. I end up sprawled in the dirt, still laughing, and I don't even know at what.

Harmony leans over me. She's laughing too. She tips some wine into my mouth. I cough and choke but I swallow most of it. I open and close my mouth like a baby bird, and she gives me another drink, then takes a drink herself.

"All gone," Harmony says, holding the bottle upside down and shaking it.

I try to put my head underneath to get whatever's left, but all I end up with is a few drops on my face.

Harmony holds the bottle like it's a baseball bat and swings, but she lets go and it goes sailing out into the dark.

I hear it shatter against something. "Strike one," I say and start laughing again.

She pulls out another cigarette and her matches. "Strike two," I say when the match flares into flame. I can barely get the words out, I'm laughing so hard.

Harmony shoves my hip with her foot. "You're drunk," she says. She blows a smoke ring and then another. I watch them spread out into nothing.

twenty-nine

Someone is using the left side of my head for a drum. I touch the side of my head. There's dirt on my hands and in my hair. I open my eyes. I'm lying on the ground. There are bits of leaves and dirt stuck to my face and something gritty in my mouth.

I sit up and the pounding in my head gets worse. I try to brush the crap out of my hair but even it hurts.

Harmony comes up the hill toward me. "Hey, you're awake," she says. She offers me a take-out cup with a straw stuck through the plastic top. "Want some? It's a root beer Slurpee."

My stomach slingshots into my throat at the thought of drinking root beer—or anything else so sweet. I shake my head, which turns out to be a very bad idea.

"You should eat something," Harmony says. "It'll help the hangover." She leans down and starts picking stuff out of my hair. "There's a Burger Doodle up the hill from here, and they stop doing breakfast at ten. If you're there at about ten after, they throw out a lot of the leftovers and they're still hot."

Breakfast out of a garbage can?

I press my fist against my stomach and feel the strap of my purse crossing my body. "I still have a little money," I say. "I can buy breakfast." There's dirt on my tongue. I pull the neck of my shirt up and try to wipe it off.

"You mean for both of us?" Harmony asks.

"Yeah," I say, getting to my feet. The ground feels wobbly, like I'm standing on a boat.

"We should go to the library first then," she says. "It's closer than the park."

"What?" I say.

"Bathrooms. You know that little park with all the trees where people skate in the winter? There's a good bathroom there at the back of the lodge. Unless you'd rather just pee behind a tree."

"No," I say. I don't want to pee behind a tree.

"Library's even better. You can get cleaned up there. They have a big bathroom in the kids section, you know, for people with babies, and crips and old people who can't use the regular bathrooms." She brushes some dirt off the back of my jacket. "C'mon, I'll show you."

She starts down the hill and I follow. At the bottom we scramble over the wall and down onto the sidewalk. But Harmony doesn't stay on the sidewalk a lot. She cuts through a lot of alleyways and dodges behind buildings. At the end of one narrow alley, she suddenly stops beside a green dumpster. "Bang on the side if anyone comes," she says.

"What do you mean?" I say, but she's already pulled herself up the side of the dumpster and is lifting one side of the top. She balances on the lip for a second and then flips inside like some kind of garbage diver. After a minute a pink sweatshirt comes flying out of the garbage, followed by a dark blue T-shirt. Then one red high-top sneaker arcs over the side and lands at my feet. A second later the matching sneaker drops by the side of the dumpster.

Harmony reappears then. She swings her legs over the edge and jumps to the ground. She looks at me. "You too much of a princess to pick things up?" she asks.

"You want this stuff?" I say. I notice she has a plastic grocery bag in one hand.

"You figure on wearing those clothes forever?" she asks. She picks up the T-shirt. "See? There's just a little hole here at the neck." She stuffs it in the bag and snags one of the shoes. "Look at this. These are barely worn but someone drew stuff all over them. Like I care."

I pick up the shoe that's in front of me. The red canvas is covered with stars and lightning bolts drawn with a black Sharpie. Harmony holds up the pink sweatshirt. "This should fit you." She points to a white blotch on one sleeve. "Only thing wrong is this bleach mark."

She takes the shoe and the shirt and jams them both in the bag. "C'mon," she says. "Let's go before someone sees us."

"What is this place?" I ask her as we walk.

"It's a store where people sell clothes they don't want anymore." Harmony doesn't look at me when she talks. She looks everywhere else, watching everything all the time. "Anything that's damaged they just throw out." She grabs my arm and pulls me down another alley. "If they catch you in the dumpster, they'll call the cops. They'd rather all that stuff be garbage."

We come out behind the main branch of the library. Inside, Harmony takes me to a washroom at the far end of the children's department. With the door locked behind us, she climbs up on the toilet, pushes back a ceiling tile and pulls down another plastic grocery bag. She rummages inside, throws a pale blue sweater over her shoulder and tosses me a long-sleeve black T-shirt and a comb. She keeps fishing in the bag. "Now where is that?" she mutters. "Oh. Here." She pulls out a big tube of toothpaste and hands it to me. "No brush. You gotta use a finger," she says with a shrug.

Harmony shoves the bag back into the hole in the ceiling and puts the other bag with the stuff she just got from the dumpster up beside it. Then she slides the square tile back in place.

"Okay, you can go first," she says, jumping down off the toilet. "I'll wait outside."

The first thing I do when the door closes behind her is pee. Then I look at myself in the spotty mirror over the sink. My head is still pounding. My face is sweaty, and there's dirt and crap in my hair.

I wash my face with cold water and soap that looks like pink foam. I comb the knots and junk out of my hair and pull it back into a ponytail. Finally I shake off my jacket and change my shirt for the one Harmony gave me. It's wrinkled but it smells clean, like bleach. I wish I had clean underwear. I wonder if Harmony gets that out of the garbage too.

I wait outside the door and watch the kids at story time while Harmony gets cleaned up. When she comes out, she's wearing the blue T-shirt with a couple of sparkly pink clips in her hair and frosted pink lipstick.

We head down the street and around the corner to a tiny diner I didn't even know was there. "This place is good," Harmony says. "The Big Breakfast has a lot of stuff and it's pretty cheap."

We sit at the counter and order two Big Breakfasts. That turns out to be scrambled eggs, a pancake, ham, fried potatoes and toast. I eat everything because suddenly I'm hungry and I don't know when I'll eat again. I haven't figured out what I'm going to do next. At least the food helps my headache.

After she's finished eating, Harmony takes a lipstick out of her pocket. There's a small mirror on the end of the cap, and she uses it to put on more shiny gloss. I look at the gold case and realize it's not some cheap dollar-store brand. "Did you find that in the dumpster?" I ask.

Harmony is playing with her bangs, squinting at the tiny mirror. "This?" she says. "Yeah, right. I picked this up at the library."

"What? Someone just left it in that bathroom?"

She laughs. "Someone just left it in their purse and, whoops, it fell out."

"You stole it?"

"Loosen up, Princess," she says, snapping the cap back on the lipstick and slipping it in her pocket again. "Stealing is when you take money. I just sorta borrowed this. She probably won't even miss it, and if she does, so what? You shoulda seen that purse. Leather was so freakin' soft. It didn't come out of a dumpster. She can afford another lipstick."

Harmony slides down off the stool. "Look, I got some stuff to do. Thanks for breakfast," she says. "I'll find you later."

She takes off and I count out enough money for the check and a small tip. I have a bit more than a hundred dollars in my purse—most of it money I conned out of my mother. I think about ordering something else just so I can stay here a bit longer, but I know I have to watch my cash.

My school ID card is tucked in the front of my wallet. I pull it out and look at the picture. I'm not her anymore. That life is over. Just the way my dad's and Seth's lives are over.

Tears fill my eyes and I swipe at them with the sleeve of my jacket because I'm not going to cry. Not here. I bend the card until it snaps in half, and I break those pieces too. I drop them all in the garbage can by the door.

I start walking back toward the library, and when I turn the corner, there they are. My mother and Marissa are standing on the sidewalk in front of the main library entrance. I back-pedal without looking where I'm going and step into a narrow alley between an art supply store and a candy shop.

They're stopping everyone who walks by. Is that my picture my mother's showing people? What's that pile of papers Marissa's holding? Flyers? What do they say? *Have You Seen This Girl?*

They want D'Arcy. I have D'Arcy's face, but that's all. Her life is over. She doesn't exist anymore. Would they understand that? Everyone D'Arcy loved is dead. Now D'Arcy is dead. Or close enough.

My mother and Marissa are looking for a dead person. I turn down the alley and walk away.

thirty

I head back to the hill and the old hospital, walking the way Harmony brought us, sticking to alleys and the back of buildings as much as I can. At the back of one old brick building, there's a row of blue recycling bins. One of them is filled with magazines and newspapers. I look around. I don't see anyone. I reach into the bin and yank out several magazines without even looking to see what they are.

Then I take off, hugging the magazines to my chest.

I don't stop for a breath until I've climbed up over the stone wall and found the path up the hill. I sit on the dried grass in the sun, with my back against the old hospital wall. The sun's already warmed the stones, and the heat soaks into my back.

I lay out the magazines. I have an issue of *People* from last week, plus *Vanity Fair* and *National Geographic* from a month ago.

I read the magazines and watch the cars go by on the street below. There's an article about Mexico in *National Geographic*. My dad went to Mexico to take pictures for a story in some other travel magazine. I'm never going to Mexico. I'm never going anywhere.

When I'm hungry again, I head down the hill and walk over to the park Harmony talked about, staying off the sidewalks as much as I can. I use the washroom and then I get something to eat at a little store across from the park that sells newspapers and cigarettes and other stuff—a wrapped sandwich with ham and pickles, a banana, a bottle of apple juice and a bag of chips.

Harmony doesn't come back until it's getting dark. "You hungry?" she asks. She's carrying a brown paper bag. There's a big grease stain on one end.

"Yeah, a little," I say.

Harmony sits, cross-legged, on the ground and opens the bag. She hands me what turns out to be a bacon cheeseburger, unwraps one for herself and pulls out a bottle of wine cooler. She takes a long drink and offers the bottle to me. I wipe the opening on my shirt, then take a drink. It's kind of sweet, but I don't really care. I turn the bottle around—*Mandarin Mango* the label says.

We finish our food, passing the wine cooler back and forth until the bottle is empty.

"That's all I have," Harmony says, setting the empty bottle spinning in the dirt. "You got any more money? I can probably get us a bottle like last night."

"I have a little left," I tell her. I take a twenty out of my purse and hand it to her, careful not to let her see how much cash I actually have.

"Let's go," Harmony says, getting to her feet.

We go back to the same place at the bend in the road. I wait, the same as I did the night before, and just like then we end up with a bottle of wine and a few cigarettes.

We walk back to our place along the old hospital foundation. "You don't mind I got a few smokes, do you?" Harmony asks.

"I don't care," I say. The warm buzzing in my head from the wine cooler is already disappearing. All I care about is the bottle.

For some reason it seems to have more in it or be lasting longer. Maybe it's a magic bottle. Maybe it's never going to be empty. I hold the bottle up and try looking down the neck. When I do that, I see two bottles. My magic bottle has split into two bottles.

"I have to pee," I tell Harmony.

She helps me partway down the hill because the magic bottle has cast an evil spell on my legs and they don't work so well. Behind a clump of alders, I manage to squat and get my pants down before I pee myself. "I'm camping," I shout to the world, flinging my arms in the air.

I fall backward and slide a few feet farther down the hill. "Olympic luge," I shout. "Go for the gold!"

Harmony helps me stand and fix my pants.

"I could do it," I say. "I could be a luger. Or is that a lugette?"

"How would I know?" Harmony says. She sets me against the wall.

I reach for the bottle, almost knocking it over. "To luging," I say, raising it high in the air before taking a drink. I fall sideways. Harmony grabs the bottle before I hit the dirt. And then there isn't anything else.

*
**

I'm puking. I feel puke on my face and my hair, and I can't get my head up. I press my hand over my mouth and vomit spews between my fingers and down my arm.

I can't...can't breathe. Can't...breathe. I try...I try to get a breath...no air...

Flashes of light go off in my head. My mouth hangs open and I'm twitching, grabbing at my throat, trying, trying to breathe.

I can't...no air...

Something, someone, kicks me hard in the back. I roll forward onto my face, vomit one more time, turn my face just a little and somehow suck in a breath.

"She's all right," a voice says from far away.

I take another rough breath and another. Finally, somehow, I manage to sit up. I wipe vomit off my face. There are clumps of puke all down my front.

It's dark. Shivering, I curl into a little ball against the wall. My head feels like it's too big for my body, and I can't keep my eyes open.

It's just beginning to get light when I wake up. My head feels like someone is beating on it with a hammer. When I move, something sharp stabs into the middle of my back. I get to my feet slowly, holding on to the brick wall.

My clothes are covered with dirt and puke. My hair is matted with dried leaves and bits of gravel. I know before I look inside my purse that all my money is gone. I feel sick.

I don't know what to do.

There's a crumpled piece of purple paper on the ground. Marissa was carrying a pile of purple papers when I saw her with my mother outside the library. Was that yesterday?

I pick the paper up and smooth it flat. The words float in front of my eyes as though they're going to sail right off the page: *SETH IS ALIVE.*

That's all it says, in big black letters. But I was at the hospital. He can't be. *He can't be.* I asked God to make it different, to make my father be alive, and he didn't. So how can Seth be alive? It's just a trick to get me to go home.

I hear the Chuck Wagon pull up. I take a couple of steps around the wall and look up the hill. The old van is there, the back doors already open.

And my mother is there, pouring coffee and showing the flyer to everyone. And then I see Marissa and Mr. Kelly and Alice from across the street in her sandals and wool socks.

I look down at the paper in my hand. My eyes swim with tears. I swipe at them with the back of my hand. I watch my mother move from person to person, slowly getting closer to where I'm standing. I should move, hide, but I don't.

She hands a cup of coffee to a girl in a long black coat, and as the girl moves away, my mother looks down the hill and sees me. She takes one step toward me, eyes on my face as though she expects me to run. Then another step. And another. She slips, puts out a hand and almost falls, but she keeps coming, scrambling down the bank to me.

Her hair isn't combed. She's wearing jeans and a heavy dark sweater with buttons. She reaches for me and I take a step backward. Her hand drops to her side. "Oh baby, I'm so glad you're all right," she says. A tear trails down her cheek. She brushes it away. "I'm sorry. I'm sorry you felt you had to run away." She lets out a breath. "I haven't done this right. I don't know how to be a family without your father. But I'm going to find out. I promise."

I don't speak. I don't move.

Mom sees the paper, crushed now in my fist. "You saw it," she says. "I was afraid you thought...He's not dead."

I make a fist and hit her forearm. "You're lying," I say.

She shakes her head. "No." I hit her shoulder with my other fist. She grabs my arm. "Seth's alive," she says.

"You're lying!" I shout, beating on her with my free hand. One punch catches her on the side of the face and her eyes fill with tears. Another lands just below the collarbone.

Somehow she manages to get both of her arms around me. She doesn't seem to care that I'm filthy and I stink. "Seth's alive," she says again.

I don't trust her. "Let me go!" I shout. I try to twist away, but she won't let go.

I hit and kick with all my strength, but she won't let go. I scrape her arm with my fingernails. She keeps holding on to me.

I can feel something raw and angry inside me trying to get out. "Why did he leave me?" I scream, and I don't know if I mean Seth or my father.

Mom holds me tight against her chest. "I'm not going to leave you. I'm not letting go," she says. "If you run away, I'll never stop looking for you. Never."

I try to pull away, but I can't fight her anymore.

"Never," she whispers again.

And then something breaks inside me. I feel a sharp pain in my chest and I sag against my mother, shaking and crying—for Seth, for my dad, for me.

Part Three

Spring

thirty-one

I think this park is the most beautiful place I have ever seen. There are trees everywhere I look. Strong, tall trees that will still be here when it's time for someone to say good-bye to me. But today we're here to say good-bye to my dad.

I push Seth's wheelchair up to the top of a rise that seems to. Have slid in just under the sky. I breathe deeper and I feel, somehow, connected to all of this.

The right side of Seth's body doesn't work the way it used to, that's why he needs the wheelchair. When he tried to kill himself, he had a stroke. He has to learn how to walk again, how to feed himself, how to write his name, how to talk. But Seth's alive, and that's all I care about. I'm teaching him how to juggle, and that makes us both laugh.

The trail ends in an open area. This is the place. A forest fire a year ago destroyed this part of the park. But I can see so many tiny green things growing again, up through the sooty ground. We're here to plant a tree for my dad, to cele-brate his life with a living thing.

I set the brake on Seth's chair. He gives me his loopy, lopsided smile and takes my hand with his good one.

Mom stands beside us, puts her arm around my shoulders, and I put mine around hers. We've talked a lot in the past few weeks—just the two of us and with a counselor too. Some of the things have been hard to say and hard to hear. But I'm learning that saying the words and living the feelings help.

And I've talked to Marissa too. I've fixed things with her. But not with Brendan. He wants the person I used to be, and I'm not that person anymore.

Overhead the sky is a deep, cloudless blue that seems to go on forever. I like to think that Dad still goes on somehow. I hate what he did, but I don't hate him. I close my eyes, and even though it feels kind of hokey, I send my love out into that endless blue, to wherever he is, whatever he is now.

Tomorrow my mother and I are going to see Claire. I don't know if we can be the family Dad wanted, but I am going to try, harder than I have ever tried at anything before.

Tomorrow I'm going to hug Claire and find out whether or not she will hug me back.

acknowledgements

Thanks to Judy Gorham, who has known me since I was a geeky teenager—and has the pictures to prove it—for always cheering me on. Thanks to Andrew Wooldridge for his excellent editing. And special thanks to Susan Evans for reading the early versions of this book and for urging me to finish it. I'm glad you're here. This book is for you.

Amyotrophic lateral sclerosis, also known as ALS or Lou Gehrig's disease, attacks nerve cells in the brain and spinal cord, causing muscle weakness, atrophy and paralysis. There is no known cure. Suicide has been called a permanent solution to a temporary problem. If you suspect someone close to you is thinking about suicide, please tell someone.

Darlene Ryan is the author of *Saving Grace*, *Responsible* and *Rules for Life*. Darlene lives in Fredericton, New Brunswick.